# *FROM STONEHENGE TO SPACE!*

When Legion signed on as a soldier of fortune he did not expect to wind up as the master of a private island. Nor did he expect to cower in the ancient Druid pits...nor fight for his life in the great hall at Okk-Hamiloth, on a planet many galaxies away.

Keith Laumer, one of the science fiction world's master storytellers, sweeps you through the far reaches of time and the vastness of outer space in this novel of retribution.

# CAST OF CHARACTERS

### LEGION
*All he wanted to do was pick up some quick cash in a petty robbery, but he ended up as a slave on another world!*

### FOSTER
*He was a victim of amnesia and couldn't remember his past—for the last 3000 years!*

### GOPE
*A powerful lord on the distant planet Vallon. Not a bad fellow once you got used to being his slave.*

### OMMODURAD
*Unequalled in power, he was the only man left on Vallon with knowledge of the people's long buried past. And he wasn't about to share it.*

### TORBU
*He was full of strength and honor, willing to lay his life on the line in securing a better future for his enslaved people.*

### RTHR
*This legendary ruler of Vallon had disappeared centuries ago, yet the enslaved masses still awaited his return.*

# A TRACE OF OF MEMORY

By
KEITH LAUMER

ARMCHAIR FICTION & MUSIC
PO Box 4369, Medford, Oregon   97501-0168

# PROLOGUE

HE opened his eyes and saw a grey wall where a red light gleamed balefully in the gloom. He lay on a utility mat on a high couch, clad in a gown of strange purple. In his arm there burned a harsh pain, and he saw on his skin the mark of the Hunters. Who could have dared?

He sat up, swung his legs over the side of the narrow cot...and saw the bodies of two men huddled on the floor, blood-splashed. Beyond, at a doorway, lay another, and another... What carnage was this? Gently he rolled the nearest body on its back—and crouched rigid in shock. Ammaerln, his friend... Not dead, but the pulse was faint, too faint. And the next corpse? That, too, wore a face that had been dear to him. And the bodies at the entry—his faithful men. All were friends!

Beyond the door the ranged shelves of a library gave back not even an echo when he called. He turned again to his dead. It was fresh death, the blood still wet. Quickly he scanned the room, saw a recording monitor against a wall. He fitted the neurodes to the dying man's temples. But for this gesture of recording his life's memories, there was nothing he could do. He must get him to a therapist and quickly. But no one answered his calls. Was he alone in these chambers of death?

He ran through the library to a great echoing hall beyond. This was not the Sapphire Palace beside the Shallow Sea.

The lines were unmistakeable: he was aboard a ship, a far-voyager. Why? How? He stood uncertain. The silence was absolute.

He crossed the Great Hall and entered the observation lounge. Here lay another dead man, by his uniform a member of the crew. He touched a knob and the great screens glowed blue. A giant crescent swam into focus, locked, soft green against the black of space. Beyond it a smaller companion hung, blue-blotched, airless. What worlds were these?

WHEN he had ranged the vast ship from end to end he knew that he alone still lived. Seven corpses, cruelly slashed, peopled the silent vessel. In the control sector the communicator lights glowed but to his call there was no answer from the strange world below.

He returned to the recording room. Ammaerln still breathed weakly. The memory recording had been completed; all that the dying man remembered of his long life was imprinted now in the silvery cylinder. It remained only to color-code the trace; that he would do on his return.

His eye was caught by a small object still projecting from an aperture at the side of the high couch where he had wakened. It was his own memory trace. So he himself had undergone the Change!

He thrust the color banded cylinder into a gown pocket—then whirled at a sound. A nest of Hunters—the swarming globes of pale light used to track down criminals—clustered at the door; then they were upon him.

Without a weapon, he was helpless. He must escape the ship—and quickly! While the suffocating horde pressed close, humming in their eagerness, he caught up the unconscious Ammaerln. The Hunters trailed him like a luminous streamer as he ran to the shuttle boat bay.

Three shuttles lay in their cradles. He groped to a switch, his head swimming with the sulphurous reek of his attackers. Light flooded the bay, driving them back. He entered the lifeboat, placed the body on a cushioned couch. Perhaps he would find help for his friend below.

It had been long since he had manned the controls of a vessel, but he had not forgotten.

THE last of life ebbed from the injured man long before they reached the planetary surface. The boat settled gently and the lock cycled. He looked out at a vista of ragged forest.

This was no civilized world. Only the landing-ring and the clearing around it showed the presence of man.

There was a hollow in the earth by a square marker block at the eastern perimeter of the clearing. He carried his friend there and placed him in it, scraped earth over the body. He lingered for a moment, then he rose and turned back toward the shuttle boat...

A dozen men, squat, bearded, wrapped in the shaggy hides of beasts, stood between him and the access ladder. The tallest among them shouted, raised a bronze sword threateningly. Others clustered at the ladder. One scrambled up, reached the top, disappeared into the boat. In a moment he reappeared at the opening and hurled down an armful of small bright objects of varied shapes and textures. Others clambered up to share the loot as the first man again vanished within the boat. But before the foremost had gained entry the port closed, shutting off a terrified cry from within the shuttle boat.

Men dropped from the ladder as it swung up. The boat rose slowly, angling toward the west, dwindling. The savages shrank back, awed.

The man watched until the tiny blue light was lost against the sky.

# CHAPTER ONE

THE ad read: "Soldier of fortune seeks companion in arms to share unusual adventure. Foster, Bos 19, Mayport."

I crumpled the newspaper and tossed it in the general direction of the wire basket beside the park bench, pushed back a slightly frayed cuff, and took a look at my bare wrist. It was just habit; the watch was in a hockshop in Tupelo, Mississippi. It didn't matter. I didn't have to know what time it was.

Across the park most of the store windows were dark along the side street. There were no people in sight; they were all home now, having dinner. As I watched, the lights blinked off in the drug store with the bottles of colored water in the window; that left the candy and cigar emporium at the end of the line. I fidgeted on the hard bench and felt for a cigarette I didn't have. I wished the old boy back of the counter would call it a day and go home. As soon as it was dark enough, I was going to rob his store.

I wasn't a full-time stick-up artist. Maybe that's why that nervous feeling was playing around under my rib cage. There was really nothing to it. The wooden door with the hardware-counter lock that would open almost as easily without a key as with one; the sardine-can metal box with the day's receipts in it; I'd be on my way to the depot with fare to Miami in my pocket ten minutes after I cracked the door. I'd learned a lot harder tricks than petty larceny back when I had a big future ahead with Army Intelligence. That was a long time ago, and I'd had a lot of breaks since then—none good.

I got up and took another turn around the park. It was a warm evening, and the mosquitos were out. I caught a whiff of frying hamburger from the Elite Cafe down the street. It reminded me that I hadn't eaten lately. There were lights on at the Commercial Hotel and one in the ticket office at the station. The local police force was still sitting on a stool at the Rexall talking to the counter girl. I could see the .38 revolver hanging down in a worn leather holster at his hip. All of a sudden, I was in a hurry to get it over with.

I took another look at the lights. All the stores were dark now. There was nothing to wait for. I crossed the street, sauntered past the cigar store. There were dusty boxes of stogies in the window, and piles of homemade fudge stacked on plates with paper doilies under them. Behind them, the interior of the store looked grim and dead. I passed, looked around, moved toward the door—

A BLACK sedan eased around the corner and pulled in to the curb. A face leaned over to look at me through lenses like the bottoms of tabasco bottles. The hot evening air stirred, and I felt my damp shirt cold against my back.

"Looking for anything in particular, Mister?" the cop said.

I just looked at him.

"Passing through town, are you?" he asked.

For some reason I shook my head.

"I've got a job here," I said. "I'm going to work—for Mr. Foster."

"What Mr. Foster?" The cop's voice was wheezy, but relentless, a voice used to asking questions.

I remembered the ad—something about an adventure. Foster, Box 19. The cop was still staring at me.

"Box nineteen," I said.

He looked me over some more, then reached across and opened the door. "Better come on down to the station house with me, Mister," he said.

At Police Headquarters, the cop motioned me to a chair, sat behind a desk, and pulled a phone to him. He dialed slowly, then swiveled his back to me to talk. Insects danced around a bare light bulb. There was an odor of stale beer and leather and unwashed bedding. I sat and listened to a radio in the distance wailing a sad song.

It was half an hour before I heard a car pull up outside. The man who came through the door was wearing a light suit that was neither new nor freshly pressed, but had that look of perfect fit and taste that only the most expensive tailoring can achieve. He moved in a relaxed way, but with a sense of power held in reserve. At first glance I thought he was in his middle thirties, but when he looked my way I saw the fine lines around the blue eyes. I got to my feet. He came over to me.

"I'm Foster," he said, and held out his hand. I shook it.

"My name's Legion," I said.

The desk sergeant spoke up. "This fellow says he come here to Mayport to see you, Mr. Foster."

Foster looked at me steadily. "That's right, Sergeant. This gentleman is considering a proposition I've made."

"Well, I didn't know, Mr. Foster," the cop said.

"I quite understand, Sergeant," Foster said. "We all feel better, knowing you're on the job."

"Well, you know," the cop said.

"We may as well be on our way then," Foster said. "If you're ready, Mr. Legion."

"Sure, I'm ready," I said. Mr. Foster said goodnight to the cop and we went out. On the pavement in front of the building I stopped.

"Thank you very much, Mr. Foster," I said. "I'll get out

of your hair now."

FOSTER had his hand on the door of a deceptively modest-looking cabriolet. I could smell the solid leather upholstery from where I stood.

"Why not come along to my place, Legion," he said. "We might at least discuss my proposition."

I shook my head. "I'm not the man for the job, Mr. Foster," I said. "If you'd like to advance me a couple of bucks, I'll get myself a bite to eat and fade right out of your life."

"What makes you so sure you're not interested?"

"Your ad said something about adventure. I've had my adventures. Now I'm just looking for a hole to crawl into."

"I don't believe you, Legion." Foster smiled at me, a slow, calm smile. "I think your adventures have hardly begun."

I thought about it. If I went along, I'd at least get a meal —and maybe even a bed for the night. It was better than curling up under a tree.

"Well," I said, "a remark like that demands time for an explanation." I got in the car and sank back in a seat that seemed to fit me like Foster's jacket fit him.

"I hope you won't mind if I drive fast," Foster said. "I want to be home before dark." We started up and wheeled away from the curb like a torpedo sliding out of the launching tube.

I GOT out of the car in the drive at Foster's house, and looked around at the wide clipped lawn, the flower beds that were vivid even by moonlight, the line of tall poplars, and the big white house.

"I wish I hadn't come," I said. "This kind of place reminds me of all the things I haven't gotten out of life."

"Your life's still ahead of you," Foster said. He opened

the slab of mahogany that was the front door, and I followed him inside. At the end of a short hall he flipped a switch that flooded the room before us with soft light. I stared at a pale grey carpet about the size of a tennis court, decked out with Danish teak upholstered in rich colors. The walls were a rough-textured grey; here and there were expensively framed abstractions. The air was cool with the heavy coolness of air conditioning. Foster crossed to a bar that looked modest in the setting, in spite of being bigger than those in most beer joints.

"Would you care for a drink?" he said.

I looked down at my limp, stained suit, and grimy cuffs.

"Look, Mr. Foster," I said. "I just realized something. If you've got a stable, I'll go sleep in it—"

Foster laughed. "Come on; I'll show you the bath."

I CAME downstairs, clean, showered, and wearing a set of Foster's clothes. I found him sitting, sipping a drink and listening to music.

"The *Liebestod*," I said. "A little gloomy, isn't it?"

"I read something else into it," Foster said. "Sit down and have a bite to eat and a drink."

I sat in one of the big soft chairs and tried not to let my hand shake as I reached for one of the sandwiches piled on the coffee table.

"Tell me something, Mr. Legion," Foster said. "Why did you come here, mention my name—if you didn't intend to see me?"

I shook my head. "It just worked out that way."

"Tell me something about yourself," Foster said.

"It's not much of a story."

"Still, I'd like to hear it."

"Well, I was born, grew up, went to school—"

"What school?"

"University of Illinois."

"What was your major?"

"Music," I answered at once.

Foster looked at me, frowning slightly.

"It's the truth," I said. "I wanted to be a conductor. The army had other ideas. I was in my last year when the draft got me. They discovered I had what they considered an aptitude for Intelligence work. I didn't mind it. I had a pretty good time for a couple of years."

"Go on," Foster said. Well, I'd had a bath and a good meal. I owed him something. If he wanted to hear my troubles, why not tell him?

"I was putting on a demonstration. A defective timer set off a charge of HE fifty seconds early on a one-minute setting. A student was killed; I got off easy with a busted eardrum and a pound or two of gravel imbedded in my back. When I got out of the hospital, the army felt real bad about letting me go—but they did. My terminal leave pay gave me a big weekend in San Francisco and set me up in business as a private investigator."

I took another long pull at a big pewter tankard of ale and went on.

"I had enough left over after the bankruptcy proceeding a few months later to get me to Las Vegas. I lost what was left and took a job with a casino operator named Gonino.

"I stayed with Gonino for nearly a year. Then one night a visiting bank clerk lost his head and shot him eight times with a .22 target pistol. I left town the same night."

I SWALLOWED some more of Foster's ale. It was the best. Foster was a pretty good egg, too.

"After that I sold used cars for a couple of months in Memphis; then I made like a life guard at Daytona; baited hooks on a thirty foot tuna boat out of Key West; all the odd jobs with low pay and no future. I spent a couple of years in Cuba; all I got out of that was two bullet scars on the left leg, and a prominent position on a CIA blacklist.

"After that things got tough. A man in my trade can't really hope to succeed in a big way without the little blue card in the plastic cover to back his play. I was headed south for the winter, and I picked Mayport to run out of money."

I stood up. "I sure enjoyed the bath, Mr. Foster, and the meal, too—not to mention the beer. I'd like real well to get in that bed upstairs and have a night's sleep just to make it complete; but I'm not interested in the job." I turned away, started across the room.

"Legion," Foster said. I turned. A beer bottle was hanging in the air in front of my face. I put a hand up fast and the bottle slapped my palm.

"Not a bad set of reflexes for a man whose adventures are all behind him," Foster said.

I tossed the bottle aside. "If I'd missed, that would have knocked my teeth out," I said angrily.

"You didn't miss—even though you're weaving a little from the beer. And a man who can feel a pint or so of beer isn't an alcoholic—so you're clean on that score."

"I didn't say I was ready for the rummy ward," I said. "I'm just not interested in your proposition—whatever it is."

"Legion," Foster said, "maybe you have the idea I put that ad in the paper last week, on a whim. The fact is, I've been running it—in one form or another—for over eight years."

I looked at him and waited.

"Not only locally—I've run it in the big-city papers, and in some of the national weekly and monthly publications. All together, I've had perhaps fifty responses."

Foster smiled wryly. "About three quarters of them were from women who thought I wanted a playmate. Several more were from men with the same idea. The few others were hopelessly unsuitable."

"That's surprising," I said. "I'd have thought you'd have brought half the nuts in the country out of the woodwork by now."

Foster looked at me, not smiling. I realized suddenly that behind the urbane facade there was a hint of tension, a trace of worry in the level blue eyes.

"I'D LIKE very much to interest you in what I have to say, Legion. I think you lack only one thing—confidence in yourself."

I gave a sort of laugh. "What are the qualifications you think I have? I'm a jack of no trades—"

"Legion, you're a man of considerable intelligence and more than a little culture; you've traveled widely and know how to handle yourself in difficult situations—or you wouldn't have survived. I'm sure your training includes techniques of entry and fact-gathering not known to the average man; and perhaps most important, although you're an honest man, you're capable of breaking the law—when necessary."

"So that's it," I said.

"No, I'm not forming a mob, Legion. As I said in the ad —this is an unusual adventure. It may—probably will— involve infringing various statutes and regulations of one sort or another. After you know the full story I'll leave you to judge whether it's justifiable."

If Foster was trying to arouse my curiosity, he was succeeding. He was dead serious about whatever it was he was planning. It sounded like something no one with good sense would want to get involved in—but on the other hand, Foster didn't look like the sort of man to do anything foolish...

"Why don't you tell me what this is all about?" I said.

"Why would a man with all this—" I waved a hand at the luxurious room—"want to pick a hobo like me out of the gutter and talk him into taking a job?"

"Your ego has taken a severe beating, Legion—that's obvious. I think you're afraid that I'll expect too much of you —or that I'll be shocked by some disclosure you may make. Perhaps if you'd forget yourself and your problems for the moment, we could reach an understanding—"

"Yeah," I said. "Just forget my problems—"

"Chiefly money problems, of course. Most of the problems of this society involve the abstraction of values that money represents."

"Okay," I said. "I've got my problems, you've got yours. Let's leave it at that."

"You feel that, because I have material comfort, my problems must of necessity be trivial ones. Tell me, Mr. Legion: have you ever known a man who suffered from amnesia?"

FOSTER crossed the room to a small writing desk, took something from a drawer, looked at me.

"I'd like you to examine this," he said.

I went over and took the object from his hand. It was a small book, with a cover of drab-colored plastic, unornamented except for an embossed design of two concentric rings. I opened the cover. The pages were as thin as tissue, but opaque, and covered with extremely fine writing in strange foreign characters. The last dozen pages were in English. I had to hold the book close to my eyes to read the minute script:

"January 19, 1710. Having come nigh to calamity with the near lofs of the key, I will henceforth keep thif journal in the Englifh tongue…"

"If this is an explanation of something, it's too subtle for me," I said.

"Legion, how old would you say I am?"

"That's a hard one," I said. "When I first saw you I would have said the late thirties, maybe. Now, frankly, you look closer to fifty."

"I can show you proof," Foster said, "that I spent the better part of a year in a military hospital in France. I awakened in a ward, bandaged to the eyes, and with no memories whatever of my life before that day. According to the records made at the time, I appeared to be about thirty years of age."

"Well," I said, "amnesia's not so unusual among war casualties. You've done well since."

Foster shook his head impatiently. "There's nothing difficult about acquiring material wealth in this society, though the effort kept me well occupied for a number of years—and diverted my thoughts from the question of my past life. The time came, however, when I had the leisure to pursue the matter. The clues I had were meager enough; the notebook I've shown you was found near me, and I had a ring on my finger." Foster held out his hand. On the middle finger was a massive signet, engraved with the same design of concentric circles I had seen on the cover of the notebook.

"I WAS badly burned; my clothing was charred. Oddly enough, the notebook was quite unharmed, though it was found among burned debris. It's made of very tough stuff."

"What did you find out?"

"In a word—nothing. No military unit claimed me. I spoke English, from which it was deduced that I was English or American—"

"They couldn't tell which, from your accent?"

"Apparently not; it appears I spoke a sort of hybrid dialect."

"Maybe you're lucky. I'd be happy to forget my first thirty years."

"I spent a considerable sum of money in my attempts to discover my past," Foster went on. "And several years of time. In the end I gave it up. And it wasn't until then that I found the first faint inkling."

"So you did find something?"

"Nothing I hadn't had all along. The notebook."

"I'd have thought you would have read that before you did anything else," I said. "Don't tell me you put it in the bureau drawer and forgot it."

"I read it, of course—what I could read of it. Only a relatively small section is in English. The rest is a cipher. And what I read seemed meaningless—quite unrelated to me. You've glanced through it; it's no more than a journal, irregularly kept, and so cryptic as to be little better than a code itself. And of course the dates; they range from the early eighteenth century through the early twentieth."

"A sort of family record, maybe," I said. "Carried on generation after generation. Didn't it mention any names, or places?"

"Look at it again, Legion," Foster said. "See if you notice anything odd—other than what we've already discussed."

I thumbed through the book again. It was no more than an inch thick, but it was heavy—surprisingly heavy. There were a lot of pages—I shuffled through hundreds of closely written sheets and yet the book was less than half used. I read bits here and there:

"May 4, 1746. The Voyage waf not a Succefs. I muft forfake thif avenue of Enquiry..."

"October 23, 1790. Builded the weft Barrier a cubit higher. Now the fires burn every night. Is there no limit to their infernal perfiftence?"

"January 19, 1831. I have great hopes for the Philadelphia

enterprise. My greatest foe is impatience. All preparations for the Change are made, yet I confess I am uneasy..."

"THERE are plenty of oddities," I said. "Aside from the entries themselves. This is supposed to be old—but the quality of the paper and binding beats anything I've seen. And that handwriting is pretty fancy for a quill pen—"

"There's a stylus clipped to the spine of the book," Foster said. "It was written with that."

I looked, pulled out a slim pen, then looked at Foster. "Speaking of odd," I said. "A genuine antique early colonial ball-point pen doesn't turn up every day—"

"Suspend your judgment until you've seen it all," Foster said.

"And two hundred years on one refill—that's not bad." I riffled through the pages, tossed the book onto the table. "Who's kidding who, Foster?" I said.

"The book was described in detail in the official record, of which I have copies. They mention the paper and binding, the stylus, even quote some of the entries. The authorities worked over it pretty closely, trying to identify me. They reached the same conclusion as you—that it was the work of a crackpot; but they saw the same book you're looking at now."

"So what? So it was faked up some time during the war —what does that prove? I'm ready to concede it's sixteen years old—"

"You don't understand, Legion," Foster said. "I told you I woke up in a military hospital in France. But it was an AEF hospital and the year was 1918."

## CHAPTER TWO

I POURED myself some more beer and glanced sideways at Foster. He didn't look like a nut...

"All I've got to say is," I said, "you're a hell of a spry-looking seventy."

"You find my appearance strangely youthful. What would be your reaction if I told you that I've aged greatly in the past few months? That a year ago I could have passed as no older than thirty without the slightest difficulty—"

"I don't think I'd believe you," I said. "And I'm sorry, Mr. Foster; but I don't believe the bit about the 1918 hospital either. How can I? It's—"

"I know. Fantastic. But let's go back a moment to the book itself. Look closely at the paper; it's been examined by experts. They're baffled by it. Attempts to analyze it chemically failed—they were unable to take a sample. It's impervious to solvents—"

"They couldn't get a sample?" I said. "Why not just tear off the corner of one of the sheets?"

"Try it," Foster said.

I picked up the book and plucked at the edge of one of the blank sheets, then pinched harder and pulled. The paper held. I got a better grip and pulled again. It was like fine, tough leather, except that it didn't even stretch.

"It's tough, all right," I said. I took out my pocketknife and opened it and worked on the edge of the paper.

20

Nothing. I went over to the bureau and put the paper flat against the top and sawed at it, putting my weight on the knife. I raised the knife and brought it down hard. I didn't so much as mark the sheet. I put the knife away.

"That's some paper, Mr. Foster," I said.

"Try to tear the binding," Foster said. "Put a match to it. Shoot at it if you like. Nothing will make an impression on that material. Now, you're a logical man, Legion. Is there something here outside ordinary experience or is there not?"

I sat down, feeling for a cigarette...I still didn't have one.

"What does it prove?" I said.

"Only that the book is not a simple fraud. You're facing something, which can't be dismissed as fancy. The book exists. That is our basic point of departure."

"Where do we go from there?"

"There is a second factor to be considered," Foster went on. "At some time in the past I seem to have made an enemy. Someone, or something, is systematically hunting me."

I TRIED a laugh, but it felt out of place. "Why not sit still and let it catch up with you? Maybe it could tell you what the whole thing is about."

Foster shook his head. "It started almost thirty years ago," he said. "I was driving south from Albany, New York, at night. It was a long straight stretch of road, no houses. I noticed lights following me. Not headlights—something that bobbed along, off in the fields along the road. But they kept pace, gradually moving alongside. Then they closed in ahead, keeping out of range of my headlights. I stopped the car. I wasn't seriously alarmed, just curious. I wanted a better look, so I switched on my spotlight and played it on the lights. They disappeared as the light touched them. After half a dozen were gone the rest began closing in. I kept picking them off. There was a sound, too, a sort of high-pitched humming. I caught a whiff of sulphur then, and suddenly I was afraid—deathly afraid. I caught the last one in the beam no more than ten feet from the car. I can't describe the horror of the moment—"

"It sounds pretty weird," I said. "But what was there to be afraid of? It must have been some kind of heat lightning."

"There is always the pat explanation," Foster said. "But no explanation can rationalize the instinctive dread I felt. I started up the car and drove on—right through the night and the next day. I sensed that I must put distance between myself and whatever it was I had met. I bought a home in California and tried to put the incident out of my mind—with limited success. Then it happened again."

"The same thing? Lights?"

"It was more sophisticated the next time. It started with interference—static—on my radio. Then it affected the wiring in the house. All the lights began to glow weakly, even though they were switched off. I could feel it—feel it in my bones—moving closer, hemming me in. I tried the car; it wouldn't start. Fortunately, I kept a few horses at that time. I mounted and rode into town—and at a fair gallop, you may be sure. I saw the lights, but out-distanced them. I caught a train and kept going."

"I don't see—"

"It happened again; four times in all. I thought perhaps I had succeeded in eluding it at last. I was mistaken. I have had definite indications that my time here is drawing to a close. I would have been gone before now, but there were certain arrangements to be made."

"Look," I said. "This is all wrong. You need a psychiatrist, not an ex-tough guy. Delusions of persecution —"

"IT seemed obvious that the explanation was to be found somewhere in my past life," Foster went on. "I turned to the notebook, my only link. I copied it out, including the encrypted portion. I had photostatic enlargements made of the initial section—the part written in unfamiliar characters. None of the experts who have examined the script have been able to identify it.

"I necessarily, therefore, concentrated my attention on the last section—the only part written in English. I was immediately struck by a curious fact I had ignored before. The writer made references to an Enemy, a mysterious 'they,' against which defensive measures had to be taken."

"Maybe that's where you got the idea," I said. "When you first read the book—"

"The writer of the log," Foster said, "was dogged by the same nemesis that now follows me."

"It doesn't make any sense," I said.

"For the moment," Foster said, "stop looking for logic in the situation. Look for a pattern instead."

"There's a pattern, all right," I said.

"The next thing that struck me," Foster went on, "was a reference to a loss of memory—a second point of some familiarity to me. The writer expresses frustration at the inability to remember certain facts which would have been useful to him in his pursuit."

"What kind of pursuit?"

"Some sort of scientific project, as nearly as I can gather. The journal bristles with tantalizing references to matters that are never explained."

"And you think the man that wrote it had amnesia?"

"Not actually amnesia, perhaps," Foster said. "But there were things he was unable to remember."

"If that's amnesia, we've all got it," I said. "Nobody's got a perfect memory."

"But these were matters of importance; not the kind of thing that simply slip one's mind."

"I can see how you'd want to believe the book had something to do with your past, Mr. Foster," I said. "It must be a hard thing, not knowing your own life story. But you're on the wrong track. Maybe the book is a story you started to write—in code, so nobody would accidentally read the stuff and kid you about it."

"Legion, what was it you planned to do when you got to Miami?"

The question caught me a little off-guard. "Well, I don't know," I hedged. "I wanted to get south, where it's warm. I used to know a few people—"

"In other words, nothing," Foster said. "Legion, I'll pay you well to stay with me and see this thing through."

I shook my head. "Not me, Mr. Foster. The whole thing sounds—well, the kindest word I can think of is 'nutty'."

"Legion," Foster said, "do you really believe I'm insane'?"

"Let's just say this all seems a little screwy to me, Mr. Foster."

"I'm not asking you just to work for me," Foster said. "I'm asking for your help."

"You might as well look for your fortune in tea leaves," I said, irritated. "There's nothing in what you've told me."

"THERE'S more, Legion. Much more. I've recently made an important discovery. When I know you're with me, I'll tell you. You know enough now to accept the fact that this isn't entirely a figment of my imagination."

"I don't know anything," I said. "So far it's all talk."

"If you're concerned about payment—"

"No, damn it," I barked. "Where are the papers you keep talking about? I ought to have my head examined for sitting here humoring you. I've got troubles enough—" I stopped talking and rubbed my hands over my scalp. "I'm sorry, Mr. Foster," I said. "I guess what's really griping me is that you've got everything I think I want—and you're not content with it. It bothers me to see you off chasing fairies. If a man with his health and plenty of money can't enjoy life, what the hell is there for anybody?"

Foster looked at me thoughtfully. "Legion, if you could have anything in life you wanted, what would you ask for?"

I swirled the beer in the mug. "Anything? I've wanted a lot of different things. Once I wanted to be a hero. Later, I wanted to be smart, know all the answers. Then I had the idea that a chance to do an honest job, one that needed doing, was the big thing. I never found that job. I never got smart either, or figured out how to tell a hero from a coward, without a program."

"In other words," Foster said, "you were looking for an abstraction to believe in—in this case, Justice. But you won't find justice in nature. It's a thing that only man expects or acknowledges."

"There are some good things in life; I'd like to get a piece of them."

"Don't lose your capacity for dreaming, in the process."

"Dreams?" I said. "Oh, I've got those. I want an island somewhere in the sun, where I can spend my time fishing and watching the sea and working my way through a carefully selected harem and an even more carefully selected wine cellar."

"You're speaking cynically—but you're still attempting to concretize an abstraction," Foster said. "But no matter—materialism is simply another form of idealism."

I looked at Foster. "But I know I'll never have those things—or that Justice you were talking about, either. Once you really know you'll never make it..."

"Perhaps unattainability is an essential element of any dream," Foster said. "But hold onto your dream, whatever it is—don't ever give it up."

"So much for philosophy," I said. "Where is it getting us?"

"You'd like to see the papers," Foster said. He fished a key ring from an inner pocket. "If you don't mind going out to the car," he said, "and perhaps getting your hands dirty, there's a strong-box welded to the frame. I keep photostats of everything there, along with my passport, emergency funds, and so on. I've learned to be ready to travel on very short notice. Lift the floorboards; you'll see the box."

"It's not all that urgent," I said. "I'll take a look in the morning—after I've caught up on some sleep. But don't get the wrong idea—it's just my knot-headed curiosity."

"Very well," Foster said. He lay back, sighed. "I'm tired, Legion," he said. "My mind is tired."

"Yeah," I said, "so is mine—not to mention other portions of my anatomy."

"Get some sleep," Foster said. "We'll talk again in the morning."

I PUSHED back the light blanket and slid out of bed. Underfoot, the rug was as thick and soft as mink. I went across to the closet and pushed the button that made the door slide aside. My old clothes were still lying on the floor where I had left them, but I had the clean ones Foster had lent me. He wouldn't mind if I borrowed them for awhile longer—it would be cheaper for him in the long run. Foster was as looney as a six-day bike racer, but there was no point in my waiting around to tell him so.

The borrowed outfit didn't include a coat. I thought of putting my old jacket on but it was warm outside and a grey pin stripe with grease spots wouldn't help the picture any. I transferred my personal belongings from the grimy clothes on the floor, and eased the door open.

Downstairs, the curtains were drawn in the living room. I could vaguely make out the outline of the bar. It wouldn't hurt to take along a bite to eat. I groped my way behind the bar, felt along the shelves, found a stack of small cans that rattled softly. Nuts, probably. I reached to put a can on the bar and it clattered against something I couldn't see. I swore silently, felt over the obstruction. It was bulky, with the cold smoothness of metal, and there were small projections with sharp corners. It felt for all the world like—

I leaned over it and squinted. With the faint gleam of moonlight from a chink in the heavy curtains falling just so, I could almost make out the shape; I crouched a little lower, and caught the glint of light along the perforated jacket of a . 30 calibre machine gun. My eye followed the barrel, made out the darker square of the entrance hall, and the tiny reflection of light off the polished brass doorknob at the far end.

I stepped back, flattened against the wall, with a hollow feeling inside. If I had tried to walk through that door...

Foster was crazy enough for two ordinary nuts. My eyes flicked around the room. I had to get out quickly before he jumped out and said Boo and I died of heart failure. The windows, maybe. I came around the end of the bar, got down and crawled under the barrel of the gun, and over to the heavy drapes, pushed them aside. Pale light glowed beyond the glass. Not the soft light of the moon, but a milky, churning glow that reminded me of the phosphorescence of sea water...

I dropped the curtain, ducked back under the gun into the hall and pushed through a swinging door into the kitchen. There was a faint glow from the luminous handle of the refrigerator. I yanked it open, spilling light on the floor, and looked around. Plenty of gleaming white fixtures—but no door out. There was a window, almost obscured by leaves. I eased it open and almost broke my fist on a wrought iron trellis.

BACK in the hall, I tried two more doors, both locked. A third opened, and I found myself looking down the cellar stairs. They were steep and dark like cellar stairs always seem to be but they might be the way out. I felt for a light switch, flipped it on. A weak illumination showed me a patch of damp-looking floor at the foot of the steps. It still wasn't inviting, but I went down.

There was an oil furnace in the center of the room, with dusty duct work spidering out across the ceiling; some heavy packing cases of rough wood were stacked along one wall, and at the far side of the room there was a boarded-up coal bin—but no cellar door.

I turned to go back up and heard a sound and froze. Somewhere a cockroach scuttled briefly. Then I heard the sound again; a faint grinding of stone against stone. I peered through the cobwebbed shadows, my mouth suddenly dry. There was nothing.

The thing for me to do was to get up the stairs fast, batter the iron trellis out of that kitchen window, and run like hell. The trouble was, I had to move to do it, and the sound of my own steps was so loud it was paralyzing. Compared to this, the shock of stumbling over the gun was just a mild kick. Ordinarily I didn't believe in things that went bump in the night, but this time I was hearing the bumps myself, and all I could think about was Edgar Allan Poe and his cheery tales about people who got themselves buried before they were thoroughly dead.

There was another sound, then a sharp snap, and I saw light spring up from a crack that opened across the floor in the shadowy corner. That was enough for me. I jumped for the stairs, took them three at a time, and banged through the kitchen door. I grabbed up a chair, swung it up, and slammed it against the trellis. It bounced back and cracked me across the mouth. I dropped it, tasting blood. Maybe that was what I needed. The panic faded before a stronger emotion—anger. I turned and barged along the dark hall to the living room—and lights suddenly went on. I whirled and saw Foster standing in the hall doorway, fully dressed.

"OK, Foster!" I yelled. "Just show me the way out of here."

Foster held my eyes, his face tense. "Calm yourself, Mr. Legion," he said softly. "What happened here?"

"Get over there to that gun," I snapped, nodding toward the .30 calibre on the bar. "Disarm it, and then get the front door open. I'm leaving."

Foster's eyes flicked over the clothes I was wearing. "So I see," he said. He looked me in the face again. "What is it that's frightened you, Legion?"

"Don't act so damned innocent," I said. "Or am I supposed to get the idea the brownies set up that booby trap while you were asleep?"

His eyes went to the gun and his expression tightened. "It's mine," he said. "It's an automatic arrangement. Something's activated it—and without sounding my alarm. You haven't been outside, have you?"

"How could I—"

"This is important, Legion," Foster rapped. "It would take more than the sight of a machine gun to panic you. What have you seen?"

"I was looking for a back door," I said. "I went down to the cellar. I didn't like it down there so I came back up."

"What did you see in the cellar?" Foster's face looked strained, colorless.

"It looked like..." I hesitated. "There was a crack in the floor, noises, lights..."

"The floor," Foster said. "Certainly. That's the weak point." He seemed to be talking to himself.

I jerked a thumb over my shoulder. "Something funny going on outside your windows, too."

FOSTER looked toward the heavy hangings. "Listen carefully, Legion," he said. "We are in grave danger—both of us. It's fortunate you arose when you did. This house, as you must have guessed by now, is something of a fortress. At this moment, it is under attack. The walls are protected by some rather formidable defense. I can't say as much for the cellar floor; it's merely three feet of ferro-concrete. We'll have to go now—very swiftly, and very quietly."

"OK—show me," I said. Foster turned and went back along the hall to one of the locked doors, pressed something. The door opened and I followed him inside a small room. He crossed to a blank wall, pressed against it. A panel slid aside—and Foster jumped back.

"God's wounds!" he gasped.

He threw himself at the wall, and the panel closed. I stood stock-still; from somewhere there was a smell like sulphur.

"What the hell goes on?" I said. My voice cracked, like it always does when I'm scared.

"That odor!" Foster said. "Quickly—the other way!"

I stepped back and Foster pushed past me and ran along the hall, with me at his heels. I didn't look back to see what was at my own heels. Foster took the stairs three at a time, pulled up short on the landing. He went to his knees, shoved back an Isfahan rug as supple as sable, and gripped a steel ring set in the floor. He looked at me, his face white.

"Invoke thy gods," he said hoarsely, and heaved at the ring. A section of floor swung up, showing the first step of a flight leading down into a black hole. Foster didn't hesitate;

he dropped his feet in, scrambled down. I followed. The stairs went down about ten feet, ending on a stone floor. There was the sound of a latch turning, and we stepped out into a larger room. I saw moonlight through a row of high windows, and smelled the fragrance of fresh night air.

"We're in the garage," Foster whispered. "Go around to the other side of the car and get in—quietly." I touched the smooth flank of the rakish cabriolet, felt my way around it, and eased the door open. I slipped into the seat and closed the door gently. Beside me, Foster touched a button and a green light glowed in the dash.

"Ready?" he said.

"Sure."

The starter whined half a turn and the engine caught, and without waiting, Foster gunned it, let in the clutch. The car leaped for the closed doors, and I ducked, then saw the doors snap aside as the low-slung car roared out into the night. We took the first turn in the drive at forty, and rounded onto the highway at sixty, tires screaming. I took a look back, and caught a glimpse of the house, its stately facade white in the moonlight—and then we were out of sight.

"What's it all about?" I called over the rush of air. The needle touched ninety, kept going.

"Later," Foster barked. I didn't feel like arguing. I watched the mirror for a few minutes, wondering where all the cops were tonight. Then I settled down in the padded seat and watched the speedometer eat up the miles.

# CHAPTER THREE

IT was nearly four-thirty and a tentative grey streak showed through the palm fronds to the east before I broke the silence.

"By the way," I said. "What was the routine with the steel shutters and the bullet-proof glass in the kitchen, and the handy home model machine gun covering the front door? Mice bad around the place, are they?"

"Those things were necessary—and more."

"Now that the short hairs along my spine have relaxed," I said, "The whole thing looks pretty silly. We've run far enough now to be able to stop and turn around and stick our tongues out."

"Not yet—not for a while."

"Why don't we just go back home," I went on, "and—"

"No!" Foster said sharply. "I want your word on that, Legion. No matter what—don't ever go near that house again."

"It'll be daylight soon," I said. "We'll feel pretty asinine about this little trip after the sun comes up, but don't worry, I won't tell anybody—"

"We've got to keep moving," Foster said. "At the next town, I'll telephone for seats on a flight from Miami."

"Hold on," I said. "You're raving. What about your house? We didn't even stick around long enough to make sure the TV was turned off. And what about passports, and money, and luggage? And what makes you think I'm going with you?"

"I've kept myself in readiness for this emergency," Foster said. "There are disposition instructions for the house on file with a legal firm in Jacksonville. There is nothing to connect me with my former life, once I've changed my name and disappeared. As for the rest—we can buy luggage in the morning. My passport is in the car; perhaps we'd better go first to Puerto Rico, until we can arrange for one for you."

"Look," I said. "I got spooked in the dark; that's all. Why not just admit we made fools of ourselves?"

Foster shook his head. "The inherent inertia of the human mind," he said. "How it fights to resist new ideas."

"The kind of new ideas you're talking about could get both of us locked up in the chuckle ward," I said.

"Legion," Foster said, "I think you'd better write down what I'm going to tell you. It's important—vitally important. I won't waste time with preliminaries. The notebook I showed you—it's in my jacket. You must read the English portion of it. Afterwards, what I'm about to say may make more sense."

"I hope you don't feel your last will and testament coming on, Mr. Foster," I said. "Not before you tell me what that was we were both so eager to get away from."

"I'll be frank with you," Foster said flatly. "I don't know."

FOSTER wheeled into the dark drive of a silent service station, eased to a stop, set the brake, and slumped back in the seat.

"Do you mind driving for a while, Legion?" he said. "I'm not feeling very well."

"Sure, I'll drive," I said. I opened the door and got out and went around to his side. Foster sat limply, eyes closed, his face drawn and strained. He looked older than he had last night—years older. The night's experiences hadn't taken anything off my age, either.

Foster opened his eyes, looked at me blankly. He seemed to gather himself with an effort. "I'm sorry," he said. "I'm not myself."

He moved over and I got in the driver's seat. "If you're sick," I said, "we'd better find a doctor."

"No, it's all right," he said blurrily. "Just keep going…"

"We're a hundred and fifty miles from Mayport now," I said.

Foster turned to me, started to say something—and slumped in a dead faint. I grabbed for his pulse; it was strong and steady. I rolled up an eyelid and a dilated pupil stared sightlessly. He was all right—I hoped. But the thing to do was get him in bed and call a doctor. We were at the edge of a small town. I let the brake off and drove slowly into town, swung around the corner and pulled in front of the sagging marquee of a rundown hotel. Foster stirred as I cut the engine.

"Foster," I said. "I'm going to get you into a bed. Can you walk?" He groaned softly and opened his eyes. They were glassy. I got out and got him to the sidewalk. He was still half out. I walked him into the dingy lobby and over to a reception counter where a dim bulb burned. I dinged the bell. It was a minute before an old man shuffled out from where he'd been sleeping. He yawned, eyed me suspiciously, looked at Foster.

"We don't want no drunks here," he said. "Respectable house."

"My friend is sick," I said. "Give me a double with bath. And call a doctor."

"What's he got?" the old man said. "Ain't contagious, is it?"

"That's what I want a doctor to tell me."

"I can't get the doc 'fore in the morning. And we got no private bathrooms."

I signed the register and we rode the open-cage elevator to the fourth floor and went along a gloomy hall to a door painted a peeling brown. It didn't look inviting; the room inside wasn't much better. There was a lot of flowered wallpaper and an old-fashioned wash stand, and two wide beds. I stretched Foster out on one. He lay relaxed, a serene expression on his face—the kind undertakers try for but never quite seem to manage. I sat down on the other bed and pulled off my shoes. It was my turn to have a tired mind. I lay on the bed and let it sink down like a grey stone into still water.

I AWOKE from a dream in which I had just discovered the answer to the riddle of life. I tried to hold onto it, but it slipped away; it always does.

Grey daylight was filtering through the dusty windows. Foster lay slackly on the broad sagging bed, a ceiling lamp with a faded fringed shade casting a sickly yellow light over him. It didn't make things any cheerier; I flipped it off.

Foster was lying on his back, arms spread wide, breathing heavily. Maybe it was only exhaustion and he didn't need a doctor after all. He'd probably wake up in a little while, raring to go. As for me, I was feeling hungry again. I'd have to have a buck or so for sandwiches. I went over to the bed and called Foster's name. He didn't move. If he was sleeping that soundly, maybe I wouldn't bother him.

I eased his wallet out of his coat pocket, took it to the window and checked it. It was fat. I took a ten, put the wallet on the table. I remembered Foster had said something about money in the car. I had the keys in my pocket. I got my shoes on and let myself out quietly. Foster hadn't moved.

Down on the street, I waited for a couple of yokels who

were looking over Foster's car to move on, then slid into the seat, leaned over and got the floorboards up. The strong box was set into the channel of the frame. I scraped the road dirt off the lock and opened it with a key from Foster's key ring, took out the contents. There was a bundle of stiffish papers, a passport, some maps—marked up—and a wad of currency that made my mouth go dry. I riffled through it; fifty grand if it was a buck.

I stuffed the papers, the money and the passport back in the box and locked it, and climbed out onto the sidewalk. A few doors down the street there was a dirty window lettered MAE'S EAT. I went in, ordered hamburgers and coffee to go, and sat at the counter with Foster's keys in front of me, and thought about the car that went with them. The passport only needed a little work on the picture to get me wherever I wanted to go, and the money would buy me my choice of islands. Foster would have a nice long nap, and then take a train home. With his dough, he'd hardly miss what I took.

THE counterman put a paper bag in front of me and I paid him and went out. I stood by the car, jingling the keys on my palm and thinking. I would be in Miami in an hour, and I knew where to go for the passport job. Foster was a nice guy, and I liked him—but I'd never have a break like this again. I reached for the car door and a voice said, "Paper, Mister?"

I jumped and looked around. A dirty-faced kid was looking at me.

"Sure," I said. I gave him a single and took the paper, flipped it open. A Mayport dateline caught my eye:

*Police Raid Hideout. A surprise raid by local police led to the discovery here today of a secret gangland fortress. Chief Chesters of the Mayport Police stated that the raid came as an aftermath of the arrival in the city yesterday of a notorious northern gang member. A number of firearms, including army-type machine guns, were seized in the raid on a house 9 miles from Mayport on the Fernandina road. The raid was said by Chief Chesters to be the culmination of a lengthy investigation. C. R. Foster, 50, owner of the property, is missing and feared dead. Police are seeking an ex-convict who visited the house last night. Chief Chesters stated that Foster may have been the victim of a gangland murder.*

I BANGED through the door to the darkened room and stopped short. In the gloom I could see Foster sitting on the edge of my bed, looking my way.

"Look at this," I yelped, flapping the paper in his face. "Now the cops are dragging the state for me—and on a murder rap at that! Get on the phone and get this thing straightened out—if you can. You and your little green men! The cops think they've stumbled on Al Capone's arsenal. You'll have fun explaining that one..."

Foster looked at me interestedly. He smiled.

"What's funny about it, Foster?" I yelled. "Your dough may buy you out, but what about me?"

"Forgive me for asking," Foster said pleasantly. "But— who are you?"

There are times when I'm slow on the uptake, but this wasn't one of them; the implications of what Foster had said hit me hard enough to make my knees go weak.

"Oh, no, Mr. Foster," I said. "You can't lose your memory again—not right now, not with the police looking for me. You're my alibi; you're the one that has to explain all the business about the guns and the ad in the paper. I just came to see about a job, remember?"

My voice was getting a little shrill. Foster sat looking at me, wearing an expression between a frown and a smile, like a credit manager turning down an application.

He shook his head slightly. "My name is not Foster."

"Look," I said. "Your name was Foster yesterday—that's all I care about. You're the one that owns the house the cops are all upset about. And you're the corpse I'm supposed to have knocked off. You've got to go to the cops with me—right now—and tell them I'm just an innocent bystander."

I went to the window and raised the shades to let some light into the room, turned back to Foster.

"I'll explain to the cops about you thinking the little men were after you—" I stopped talking and stared at Foster. For a wild moment I thought I'd made a mistake—that I'd wandered into the wrong room. I knew Foster's face, all right; the light was bright enough now to see clearly; but the man I was talking to couldn't have been a day over twenty years old.

I went close to him, staring hard. There were the same cool blue eyes, but the lines around them were gone. The black hair grew lower and thicker than I remembered it, and the skin was clear and vibrant.

I sat down hard on my bed. "Mama mia," I said.

"*Que es la dificultad?*" Foster said.

"Shut up," I moaned. "I'm confused enough in one language." I was trying hard to think but I couldn't seem to get started. A few minutes earlier I'd had the world by the tail—just before it turned around and bit me. Cold sweat popped out on my forehead when I thought about how close I had come to driving off in Foster's car; every cop in the state would be looking for it by now—and if they found me in it, the jury wouldn't be ten minutes reaching a verdict of guilty.

Then another thought hit me—the kind that brings you bolt upright with your teeth clenched and your heart hammering. It wouldn't be long before the local hick cops would notice the car out front. They'd come in after me and I'd tell them it belonged to Foster. They'd take a look at him and say, nuts, the bird we want is fifty years old, and where did you hide the body?

I got up and started pacing. Foster had already told me there was nothing to connect him with his house in Mayport; the locals there had seen enough of him to know he was pushing middle age, at least. I could kick and scream and tell them this twenty-year-old kid was Foster, but I'd never make it stick. There was no way to prove my story; they'd figure Foster was dead and that I'd killed him—and anybody who thinks you need a *corpus* to prove murder better read his Perry Mason again.

I glanced out of the window and did a double take. Two cops were standing by Foster's car. One of them went around to the back and got out a pad and took down the license number, then said something over his shoulder and started across the street. The second cop planted himself by the car, his eye on the front of the hotel.

I whirled on Foster. "Get your shoes on," I croaked. "Let's get the hell out of here."

We went down the stairs quietly and found a back door opening on an alley. Nobody saw us go.

AN hour later, I sagged in a grimy coach seat and studied Foster, sitting across from me—a middle-aged nut with the face of a young kid and a mind like a blank slate. I had no choice but to drag him with me; my only chance was to stick close and hope he got back enough of his memory to get me off the hook.

It was time for me to be figuring my next move. I thought about the fifty thousand dollars I had left behind in the car, and groaned. Foster looked concerned.

"Are you in pain?" he said.

"And how I'm in pain," I said. "Before I met you I was a homeless bum, broke and hungry. Now I can add a couple more items: the cops are after me, and I've got a mental case to nursemaid."

"What law have you broken?" Foster said.

"None, damn it," I barked. "As a crook, I'm a washout. I've planned three larcenies in the last twelve hours, and flunked out on all of them. And now I'm wanted for murder."

"Whom did you kill?" Foster enquired courteously.

I leaned across so I could snarl in his face: "You!" Then, "Get this through your head, Foster. The only crime I'm guilty of is stupidity. I listened to your crazy story; because of you I'm in a mess I'll never get straightened out." I leaned back. "And then there's the question of old men that take a nap and wake up in their late teens; we'll go into that later, after I've had my nervous breakdown."

"I'm sorry if I've been the cause of difficulty," Foster said. "I wish that I could recall the things you've spoken of. Is there anything I can do to assist you now?"

"And you were the one who wanted help," I said. "There is one thing; let me have the money you've got on you; we'll need it."

Foster got out his wallet, after I told him where it was, and handed it to me. I looked through it; there was nothing in it with a photo or fingerprints. When Foster said he had arranged matters so that he could disappear without a trace, he hadn't been kidding.

"We'll go to Miami," I said. "I know a place in the Cuban section where we can lie low, cheap. Maybe if we wait a while, you'll start remembering things."

"Yes," Foster said. "That would be pleasant."

"You haven't forgotten how to talk, at least," I said. "I wonder what else you can do. Do you remember how you made all that money?"

"I can remember nothing of your economic system,"

Foster said. He looked around. "This is a very primitive world, in many respects. It should not be difficult to amass wealth here."

"I never had much luck at it," I said. "I haven't even been able to amass the price of a meal."

"Food is exchanged for money?" Foster asked.

"Everything is exchanged for money," I said. "Including most of the human virtues."

"This is a strange world," Foster said. "It will take me a long while to become accustomed to it."

"Yeah, me, too," I said. "Maybe things would be better on Mars."

Foster nodded. "Perhaps," he said. "Perhaps we should go there."

I groaned, then caught myself. "No, I'm not in pain," I said. "But don't take me so literally, Foster."

We rode along in silence for a while.

"Say, Foster," I said. "Have you still got that notebook of yours?"

Foster tried several pockets, came up with the book. He looked at it, turned it over, frowning.

"You remember it?" I said, watching him.

He shook his head slowly, then ran his finger around the circles embossed on the cover.

"This pattern," he said. "It signifies…"

"Go on, Foster," I said. "Signifies what?"

"I'm sorry," he said. "I don't remember."

I took the book and sat looking at it. It wouldn't do any good to turn myself in and tell them the whole story; they wouldn't believe me, and I wouldn't blame them. I didn't really believe it myself, and I'd lived through it. But then, maybe I was just imagining that Foster looked younger. After all, a good night's rest—

I looked at Foster, and almost groaned again. Twenty was

41

stretching it; eighteen was more like it. I was willing to swear he'd never shaved in his life.

"Foster," I said. "It's got to be in this book. Who you are, where you came from— It's the only hope I've got."

"I suggest we read it, then," Foster said.

"A bright idea," I said. "Why didn't I think of that?" I thumbed through the book to the section in English and read for an hour. Starting with the entry dated January 19, 1710, the writer had scribbled a few lines every few months. He seemed to be some kind of pioneer in the Virginia Colony. He bitched about prices, and the Indians, and the ignorance of the other settlers, and every now and then threw in a remark about the Enemy. He often took long trips, and when he got home, he bitched about those, too.

"It's a funny thing, Foster," I said. "This is supposed to have been written over a period of a couple of hundred years, but it's all in the same hand. That's kind of odd, isn't it?"

"Why should a man's handwriting change?" Foster said.

"Well, it might get a little shaky there toward the last, don't you agree?"

"Why is that?"

"I'll spell it out, Foster," I said. "Most people don't live that long. A hundred years is stretching it, to say nothing of two."

"This must be a very violent world, then," Foster said.

"Skip it," I said. "You talk like you're just visiting. By the way; do you remember how to write?"

Foster looked thoughtful. "Yes," he said. "I can write."

I handed him the book and the stylus. "Try it," I said. Foster opened to a blank page, wrote, and handed the book back to me.

"Always and always and always," I read.

I looked at Foster. "What does that mean?" I looked at the words again, then quickly flipped to the pages written in

English. I was no expert on penmanship, but this came up and cracked me right in the eye.

The book was written in Foster's hand.

IT doesn't make sense," I was saying for the fortieth time. Foster nodded sympathetic agreement.

"Why would you write this yourself, then spend time and money having it deciphered? You said experts worked on it and couldn't break it. But," I went on, "you must have known you wrote it; you knew your own handwriting. But on the other hand, you had amnesia before; you had the idea you might have told something about yourself in the book…"

I sighed, leaned back and tossed the book over to Foster. "Here, you read awhile," I said. "I'm arguing with myself and I can't tell who's winning."

Foster looked the book over carefully.

"This is odd," he said.

"What's odd?"

"The book is made of khaff. It is a permanent material—and yet it shows damage."

I sat perfectly still and waited.

"Here on the back cover," Foster said. "A scuffed area. Since this is khaff, it cannot be an actual scar. It must have been placed there."

I grabbed the book and looked. There was a faint mark across the back cover, as though the book had been scraped on something sharp. I remembered how much luck I had had with a knife. The mark had been put here, disguised as a casual nick in the finish. It had to mean something.

"How do you know what the material is?" I asked.

Foster looked surprised. "In the same way that I know the window is of glass," he said. "I simply know."

"Speaking of glass," I said. "Wait till I get my hands on a microscope. Then maybe we'll begin to get some answers."

# CHAPTER FOUR

THE two-hundred pound senorita put a pot of black Cuban coffee and a pitcher of salted milk down beside the two chipped cups, leered at me in a way that might have been appealing thirty years before, and waddled back to the kitchen. I poured a cup, gulped half of it, and shuddered. In the street outside the cafe a guitar cried *Estrellita*.

"Okay, Foster," I said. "Here's what I've got: The first half of the book is in pot-hooks—I can't read that. But this middle section: the part coded in regular letters—it's actually encrypted English. It's a sort of resume of what happened." I picked up the sheets of paper on which I had transcribed my deciphering of the coded section of the book, using the key that had been micro-engraved in the fake scratch on the back cover.

I read:

For the first time, I am afraid. My attempt to construct the communicator called down the Hunters upon me. I made such a shield as I could contrive, and sought their nesting place.

I came there and it was in that place that I knew of old, and it was no hive, but a pit in the ground, built by men of the Two Worlds. And I would have come into it, but the Hunters swarmed in their multitudes. I fought them and killed many, but at the last I fled away. I came to the western shore, and there I hired bold sailors and a poor craft, and set forth.

In forty-nine days we came to shore in this wilderness, and here were men as from the dawn of time, and I fought them, and when they had learned fear, I lived among them in peace, and the Hunters have not found this place. Now it may be that my saga ends here, but I will do what I am able.

The Change may soon come upon me; I must prepare for the stranger who will come after me. All that he must know is in these pages. And I say to him:

*"Have patience, for the time of this race draws close. Venture not again on the Eastern continent, but wait, for soon the Northern sailors must come in numbers into this wilderness. Seek out their cleverest metal-workers, and when it may be, devise a shield, and only then return to the pit of the Hunters. It lies in the plain, 50/10,000-parts of the girth of this (?) to the west of the Great Chalk Face, and 1470 parts north from the median line, as I reckon. The stones mark it well with the sign of the Two Worlds."*

I LOOKED across at Foster. "It goes on then with a blow-by-blow account of dealings with aborigines. He was trying to get them civilized in a hurry. They figured he was a god and he set them to work building roads and cutting stone and learning mathematics and so on. He was doing all he could to set things up so this stranger who was to follow him would know the score, and carry on the good work."

Foster's eyes were on my face. "What is the nature of the Change he speaks of?"

"He never says—but I suppose he's talking about death," I said. "I don't know where the stranger is supposed to come from."

"Listen to me, Legion," Foster said. There was a hint of the old anxious look in his eyes. "I think I know what the Change was. I think he knew he would forget—"

"You've got amnesia on the brain, old buddy," I said.

"—and the stranger is—himself. A man without a memory."

I sat frowning at Foster. "Yeah, maybe," I said. "Go on."

"And he says that all that the stranger needs to know is there—in the book."

"Not in the part I decoded." I said. "He describes how they're coming along with the road-building job, and how the new mine panned out—but there's nothing about what the Hunters are, or what had gone on before he tangled with them the first time."

"It must be there, Legion; but in the first section, the part written in alien symbols."

"Maybe," I said. "But why the hell didn't he give us a key to that part?"

"I think he assumed that the stranger—himself—would remember the old writing," Foster said. "How could he know that it would be forgotten with the rest?"

"Your guess is as good as any," I said. "Maybe better; you know how it feels to lose your memory."

"But we've learned a few things," Foster said. "The pit of the Hunters—we have the location."

"If you call this 'ten-thousand parts to the west of the chalk face' a location," I said.

"We know more than that," Foster said. "He mentions a plain: and it must lie on a continent to the east—"

"If you assume that he sailed from Europe to America, then the continent to the east would be Europe," I said. "But maybe he went from Africa to South America, or—"

"The mention of Northern sailors—that suggests the Vikings—"

"You seem to know a little history, Foster," I said. "You've got a lot of odd facts tucked away."

"We need maps," Foster said. "We'll look for a plain near

the sea—"

"Not necessarily."

"—and with a formation called a chalk face to the east."

"What's this 'median line' business mean?" I said. "And the bit about ten thousand parts of something?"

"I don't know," Foster said. "But we must have maps."

"I bought some this afternoon," I said. "I also got a dime-store globe. I thought we might need them. What the hell! let's, get out of this and back to the room, where we can spread out. I know it's a grim prospect, but..." I got to my feet, dropped some coins on the table and led the way out.

IT was a short half block to the flea trap we called home. The roaches scurried as we passed up the dark stairway to our not much brighter room. I crossed to the bureau and opened a drawer.

"The globe," Foster said, taking it in his hands. "I wonder if perhaps he meant a ten-thousandth part of the circumference of the earth?"

"What would he know about—"

"Disregard the anachronistic aspect of it," Foster said. "The man who wrote the book knew many things. We'll have to start with some assumptions. Let's make the obvious ones: that we're looking for a plain on the west coast of Europe, lying—" He pulled a chair up to the scabrous table and riffled through to one of my scribbled sheets: "50/10,000s of the circumference of the earth—that would be about 125 miles—west of a chalk formation, and 3675 miles north of a median line..."

"Maybe," I said, "he means the Equator."

"Certainly," Foster said. "Why not? That would mean our plain lies on a line through—" he studied the small globe. "Warsaw, and south of Amsterdam."

"But this bit about a rock outcropping," I said. "How do

47

we find out if there's any conspicuous chalk formation there?"

"We can consult a geology text," Foster said. "There may be a library nearby."

"The only chalk deposits I ever heard about," I said, "are the white cliffs of Dover."

"White cliffs…"

We both reached for the globe at once.

"125 miles west of the chalk cliffs," Foster said. He ran a finger over the globe. "North of London, but south of Birmingham. That puts us reasonably near the sea—"

"Where's that atlas?" I said. I rummaged, came up with a cheap tourists' edition, flipped the pages.

"Here's England," I said. "Now we look for a plain."

Foster put a finger on the map. "Here," he said. "A large plain—called Salisbury."

"Large is right," I said. "It would take years to find a stone cairn on that. We're getting excited about nothing. We're looking for a hole in the ground, hundreds of years old —if this lousy notebook means anything—maybe marked with a few stones—in the middle of miles of plain. And it's all guesswork anyway…" I took the atlas, turned the page.

"I don't know what I expected to get out of decoding those pages," I said. "But I was hoping for more than this."

"I think we should try, Legion," Foster said. "We can go there, search over the ground. It would be costly, but not impossible. We can start by gathering capital—"

"Wait a minute, Foster," I said. I was staring at a larger-scale map showing southern England. Suddenly my heart was thudding. I put a finger on a tiny dot in the center of Salisbury Plain.

"Six, two and even," I said. "There's your Pit of the Hunters…"

Foster leaned over, read the fine print.

"Stonehenge."

I READ from the encyclopedia page:

"*—this great stone structure, lying on the Plain of Salisbury, Wiltshire, England, is preeminent among megalithic monuments of the ancient world.*

"*Within a circular ditch 300' in diameter, stones up to 22' in height are arranged in concentric circles. The central altar stone, over 16' long, is approached from the northeast by a broad roadway called the Avenue —*"

"It is not an altar," Foster said.

"How do you know?"

"Because—" Foster frowned. "I know, that's all."

"The journal said the stones were arranged in the sign of the Two Worlds," I said. "That means the concentric circles, I suppose; the same thing that's stamped on the cover of the notebook."

"And the ring," Foster said.

"Let me read the rest," I said.

"*A great sarsen stone stands upright in the Avenue; the axis through the two stones, when erected, pointed directly to the rising of the sun on Midsummer day. Calculations based on this observation indicate a date of approximately 1600 B. C.*"

Foster took the book and I sat on the windowsill and looked out at a big Florida moon. I lit a cigarette, dragged on it, and thought about a man who long ago had crossed the North Atlantic in a dragon boat to be a god among the Indians. I wondered where he came from, and what it was he was looking for, and what kept him going in spite of the hell that showed in the spare lines of the journal he kept. If, I reminded myself, he had ever existed…

FOSTER was pouring over the book. "Look," I said. "Let's get back to earth. We have things to think about, plans to make. The fairy tales can wait until later."

"What do you suggest?" Foster said. "That we forget the things you've told me, and the things we've read here, discard the journal, and abandon the attempt to find the answers?"

"No," I said. "I'm no sorehead. Sure, there's some things here that somebody ought to look into—some day. But right now what I want is the cops off my neck. And I've been thinking. I'll dictate a letter; you write it—your lawyers know your handwriting. Tell them you were on the thin edge of a nervous breakdown—that's why all the artillery around your house—and you made up your mind suddenly to get away from it all. Tell them you don't want to be bothered, that's why you're travelling incognito, and that the northern mobster that came to see you was just stupid, not a killer. That ought to at least cool off the cops—"

Foster looked thoughtful. "That's an excellent suggestion," he said. "Then we need merely to arrange for passage to England, and proceed with the investigation."

"You don't get the idea," I said. "You can arrange things by mail so we get our hands on that dough of yours—"

"Any such attempt would merely bring the police down on us," Foster said. "You've already pointed out the unwisdom of attempting to pass myself off as—myself."

"There ought to be a way…" I said.

"We have only one avenue of inquiry," Foster said. "We have no choice but to explore it. We'll take passage on a ship to England—"

"What'll we use for money—and papers? It would cost hundreds. Unless—" I added, "—we worked our way. But that's no good. We'd still need passports—plus union cards and seamen's tickets."

"Your friend," Foster said. "The one who prepares passports. Can't he produce the other papers as well?"

"Yeah," I said. "I guess so. But it will cost us."

"I'm sure we can find a way to pay," Foster said. "Will
you see him—early in the morning?"

I looked around the blowsy room. Hot night air stirred a
geranium wilting in a tin can on the windowsill. An odor of
bad cooking and worse plumbing floated up from the street.

"At least," I said, "it would mean getting out of here."

## CHAPTER FIVE

IT was almost sundown when Foster and I pushed
through the door to the saloon bar at the Ancient Sinner and
found a corner table. I ordered a pint of mild-and-bitter and
watched Foster spread out his maps and papers. Behind us,
there was a murmur of conversation, and the thump of darts
against a board.

"When are you going to give up and admit we're wasting
our time?" I said. "Two weeks of tramping over the same
ground, and we end up in the same place; sitting in a country
pub drinking warm beer."

"We've hardly begun our investigation," Foster said
mildly.

"You keep saying that," I said. "But if there ever was
anything in that rock-pile, it's long gone. The archaeologists
have been digging over the site for years, and they haven't

come up with anything."

"They didn't know what to look for," Foster said. "They were searching for indications of religious significance, human sacrifice—that sort of thing."

"We don't know what we're looking for either," I said. "Unless you think maybe we'll meet the Hunters hiding under a loose stone."

"You say that sardonically," Foster said. "But I don't consider it impossible."

"I know," I said. "You've convinced yourself that the Hunters were after us back at Mayport when we ran off like a pair of idiots."

"From what you've told me of the circumstances—" Foster began.

"I know; you don't consider it impossible. That's the trouble with you; you don't consider anything impossible. It would make life a lot easier for me if you'd let me rule out a few items—like leprechauns who hang out at Stonehenge."

Foster looked at me, half-smiling. It had only been a few weeks since he woke up from a nap looking like a senior class president who hadn't made up his mind whether to be a preacher or a movie star but he had already lost that mild, innocent air. He learned fast, and day by day I had seen his old personality reemerge and—in spite of my attempts to hold onto the ascendency—dominate our partnership.

"It's a failing of your culture." Foster said, "that hypothesis becomes dogma almost overnight. You're too close to your neolithic, when the blind acceptance of tribal lore had survival value. Having learned to evoke the fire god from sticks, by rote, you tend to extend the principle to all 'established facts'."

"Here's an established fact for you," I said. "We've got fifteen pounds left—that's about forty dollars. It's time we figured out where to go from here, before somebody starts checking up on those phoney papers of ours."

Foster shook his head. "I'm not satisfied that we've exhausted the possibilities here. I've been studying the geometric relationships between the various structures; I have some ideas I want to check. I think it might be a good idea to go out at night, when we can work without the usual crowd of tourists observing every move. We'll have a bite to eat here and wait until dark to start out."

THE publican brought us plates of cold meat and potato salad. I worked on a thin but durable slice of ham and thought about all the people, somewhere, who were sitting down now to gracious meals in the glitter of crystal and silver. I was getting farther from my island all the time— And it was nobody's fault but mine.

"The Ancient Sinner," I said. "That's me."

Foster looked up. "Curious names these old pubs have," he said. "I suppose in some cases the origins are lost in antiquity."

"Why don't they think up something cheery," I said. "Like 'The Paradise Bar and Grill' or 'The Happy Hour Cafe'. Did you notice the sign hanging outside?"

"No."

"A picture of a skeleton. He's holding one hand up like a Yankee evangelist prophesying doom. You can see it through the window there."

Foster turned and looked out at the weathered sign creaking in the evening wind. He looked at it for a long time. There was a strange look around his eyes.

"What's the matter—?" I started.

Foster ignored me, waved to the proprietor, a short fat countryman. He came over to the table, wiping his hands on his apron.

"A very interesting old building," Foster said. "We've

been admiring it. When was it built?"

"Well, sir," the publican said. "This here house is a many a hundred year old. It were built by the monks, they say, from the monastery what used to stand nearby here. It were tore down by the king's men, Henry, that was, what time he drove the papists out."

"That would be Henry the Eighth, I suppose?"

"Aye, it would that. And this house is all that were spared, it being the brewing-house, as the king said were a worthwhile institution, and he laid on a tithe, that two kegs of stout was to be laid by for the king's use each brewing time."

"Very interesting," Foster said. "Is the custom still continued?"

The publican shook his head. "It were ended in my granfer's time, it being that the queen were a tee-totaller."

"How did it acquire the curious name—'the Ancient Sinner'?"

"The tale is," the publican said, "that one day a lay brother of the order were digging about yonder on the plain by the great stones, in search of the Druid's treasure, albeit the Abbott had forbid him to go nigh the heathen ground, and he come on the bones of a man, and being of a kindly turn, he had the thought to give them Christian burial. Now, knowing the Abbott would nae permit it, he set to work to dig a grave by moonlight in holy ground, under the monastery walls. But the Abbott, being wakeful, were abroad and come on the brother a-digging, and when he asked the why of it, the lay brother having visions of penances to burden him for many a day, he ups and tells the Abbott it were a ale cellar he were about digging, and the Abbott, not being without wisdom, clapped him on the back, and went on his way. And so it was the ale-house got built, and blessed by the Abbott, and with it the bones that was laid away under the floor beneath the ale-casks."

"SO the ancient sinner is buried under the floor?"

"Aye, so the tale goes, though I've not dug for him meself. But the house has been knowed by the name these four hundred year."

"Where was it you said the lay brother was digging?"

"On the plain yonder, by the Druid's stones, what they call Stonehenge," the publican said. He picked up the empty glasses. "What about another, gentlemen?"

"Certainly," Foster said. He sat quietly across from me, his features composed—but I could see there was tension under the surface calm.

"What's this all about?" I asked softly. "When did you get so interested in local history?"

"Later," Foster murmured. "Keep looking bored."

"That'll be easy," I said. The publican came back, placed heavy glass mugs before us.

"You were telling us about the lay brother finding the bones," Foster said. "You say they were buried in Stonehenge?"

The publican cleared his throat, glanced sideways at Foster.

"The gentlemen wouldna be from the University now, I suppose?" he said.

"Let's just say," Foster said easily, smiling, "that we have a great interest in these bits of lore—an interest supported by modest funds, of course."

The publican made a show of wiping at the rings on the table top.

"A costly business, I wager," he said. "Digging about in odd places and all. Now, knowing where to dig; that's important, I'll be bound."

"Very important," Foster said.

"Worth five pounds, easily."

"Twere my granfer told me of the spot; took me out by moonlight, he did, and showed me where his granfer had showed him. Told me it were a fine great secret, the likes of which a simple man could well take pride in."

"And an additional five pounds as a token of my personal esteem," Foster said.

The publican eyed me. "Well, a secret as was handed down father to son..."

"And, of course, my associate wishes to express his esteem, too," Foster said. "Another five pounds worth."

"That's all the esteem the budget will bear, Mr. Foster," I said. I got out the fifteen pounds and passed the money across to him. "I hope you haven't forgotten those people back home who wanted to talk to us. They'll be getting in touch with us any time now, I'll bet."

FOSTER rolled up the bills and held them in his hand. "That's true, Mr. Legion," he said. "Perhaps we shouldn't take the time..."

"But being it's for the advancement of science," the publican said, "I'm willing to make the sacrifice."

"We'll want to go out tonight," Foster said. "We have a very tight schedule."

The landlord dickered with Foster for another five minutes before he agreed to guide us to the spot where the skeleton had been found, as soon as the pub was closed for the night. He took the money and went back to the bar.

"Now tell me," I began.

"Look at the sign-board again," Foster said. I looked. The skull smiled, holding up a hand.

"I see it," I said. "But it doesn't explain why you handed over our last buck—"

"Look at the hand," Foster said. "Look at the ring on the finger."

I looked again. A heavy ring was painted on the bony index finger, with a pattern of concentric circles. It was a duplicate of the one on Foster's finger.

"Don't drink too much," Foster said. "You may need your wits about you tonight."

THE publican pulled the battered Morris Minor to the side of the highway and set the brake.

"This is as close as we best take the machine," he said. We got out, looked across the rolling plain where the megaliths of Stonehenge loomed against the last glow of sunset.

The publican rummaged in the boot, produced a ragged blanket and two long four-cell flashlights, gave one to Foster and the other to me. "Do nae use the electric torches until I tell ye," he said, "lest the whole county see there's folks abroad here." We watched as he draped the blanket over a barbed-wire fence, clambered over, and started across the barren field. Foster and I followed, not talking.

The plain was deserted. A lonely light showed on a distant slope. It was a dark night with no moon. I could hardly see the ground ahead. A car moved along a distant road, its headlights bobbing.

We moved past the outer ring of stones, skirting fallen slabs twenty feet long.

"We'll break our necks," I said. "Let's have one of the flashlights."

"Not yet," Foster whispered.

Our guide paused; we came up to him.

"It were a mortal long time since I were last hereabouts," he said. "I best take me bearings off the Friar's Heel..."

"What's that?"

"Yon great stone, standing alone in the Avenue." We squinted; it was barely visible as a dark shape against the sky.

"The bones were buried there?" Foster asked.

"Nay; all by theirself, they was. Now it were twenty paces, granfer said, him bein fifteen stone and long in the leg..." The publican muttered.

"What's to keep him from just pointing to a spot after awhile," I said to Foster, "and saying 'This is it'?"

"We'll wait and see," Foster said.

"They were a hollow, as it were, in the earth," the publican said, "with a bit of stone by it. I reckon it were fifty paces from here—" he pointed, "—yonder!'

"I don't see anything," I said.

"Let's take a closer look." Foster started off and I followed, the publican trailing behind. I made out a dim shape, with a deep depression in the earth before it.

"This could be the spot," Foster said. "Old graves often sink—"

SUDDENLY he grabbed my arm, "Look...!"

The surface of the ground before us seemed to tremble, then heave. Foster snapped on his flashlight. The earth at the bottom of the hollow rose, cracked open. A boiling mass of lumiself, rose, bumbling along the face of the weathered stone.

"Saints preserve us," the publican said in a choked voice. Foster and I stood, rooted to the spot, watching. The lone globe rose higher—and abruptly shot straight toward us. Foster threw up an arm and ducked. The ball of light veered, struck him a glancing blow and darted off a few yards, hovered. In an instant, the air was alive with the spheres, boiling up from the ground, and hurtling toward us, buzzing like a hive of yellow-jackets. Foster's flashlight lanced out toward the swarm.

"Use your light, Legion!" he shouted hoarsely. I was still standing, frozen. The globes rushed straight at Foster, ignoring me. Behind me, I heard the publican turn and run. I fumbled with the flashlight switch, snapped it on, swung the beam of white light on Foster. The globe at his head vanished as the light touched it. More globes swarmed to Foster—and popped like soap bubbles in the flashlight's glare —but more swarmed to take their place. Foster reeled, fighting at them. He swung the light—and I heard it smash against the stone behind him. In the instant darkness, the globes clustered thick around his head.

"Foster," I yelled, "run!"

He got no more than five yards before he staggered, went to his knees. "Cover," he croaked. He fell on his face. I rushed the mass of darting globes, took up a stance straddling his body. A sulphurous reek hung around me. I coughed, concentrated on beaming the lights around Foster's head. No more were rising from the crack in the earth now. A suffocating cloud pressed around both of us, but it was Foster they went for. I thought of the slab; if I could get my back to it, I might have a chance. I stooped, got a grip on Foster's coat, and started back, dragging him. The lights boiled around me. I swept the beam of light and kept going until my back slammed against the stone. I crouched against it. Now they could only come from the front.

I glanced at the cleft the lights had come from. It looked big enough to get Foster into. That would give him some protection. I tumbled him over the edge, then flattened my back against the slab and settled down to fight in earnest.

I worked in a pattern, sweeping vertically, then horizontally. The globes ignored me, drove toward the cleft, fighting to get at Foster, and I swept them away as they came. The cloud around me was smaller now, the attack less ravenous. I picked out individual globes, snuffed them out. The hum became ragged, faltered. Then there were only a few globes around me, milling wildly, disorganized. The last half dozen fled, bumbling away across the plain.

I slumped against the rock, sweat running down into my eyes, my lungs burning with the sulphur.

"Foster," I gasped. "Are you all right?"

He didn't answer. I flashed the light onto the cleft. It showed me damp clay, a few pebbles.

Foster was gone.

# CHAPTER SIX

I SCRAMBLED to the edge of the pit, played the light around inside. It shelved back at one side, and a dark mouth showed, sloping down into the earth: the hiding place the globes had swarmed from.

Foster was wedged in the opening. I scrambled down beside him, tugged him back to level ground. He was still breathing; that was something.

I wondered if the pub owner would come back, now that the lights were gone—or if he'd tell someone what had happened, bring out a search party. Somehow, I doubted it. He didn't seem like the type to ask for trouble with the ghosts of ancient sinners.

Foster groaned, opened his eyes. "Where are...they?" he muttered.

"Take it easy, Foster," I said. "You're OK now."

"Legion," Foster said. He tried to sit up. "The Hunters..."

"I worked them over with the flashlights. They're gone."

"That means..."

"Let's not worry about what it means. Let's just get out of here."

"The Hunters—they burst out of the ground—from a cleft in the earth."

"That's right. You were halfway into the hole. I guess that's where they were hiding."

"The Pit of the Hunters," Foster said.

"If you say so," I said. "Lucky you didn't go down it."

"Legion, give me the flashlight."

"I feel something coming on that I'm not going to like," I said, I handed him the light and he flashed it into the tunnel mouth. I saw a polished roof of black glass arching four feet over the rubble-strewn bottom of the shaft. A stone, dislodged by my movement, clattered away down the $30^0$ slope.

"That tunnel's man-made," I said, "And I don't mean neolithic man."

"Legion, we'll have to see what's down there," Foster said.

"We could come back later, with ropes and big insurance policies," I said.

"But we won't," said Foster. "We've found what we were looking for—"

"Sure," I said, "and it serves us right. Are you sure you feel good enough to make like Alice and the White Rabbit?"

"I'm sure. Let's go."

FOSTER thrust his legs into the opening, slid over the edge, disappeared. I followed him. I eased down a few feet, glanced back for a last look at the night sky, then lost my grip and slid. I hit bottom hard enough to knock the wind out of me, and found myself lying on a level floor.

"What is this place?" I dug the flashlight out of the rubble, flashed it around. We were in a low-ceilinged room ten yards square. I saw smooth walls, the dark bulks of massive shapes that made me think of sarcophagi in Egyptian burial vaults— except that these threw back highlights from dials and levers.

"For a couple of guys who get shy in the company of cops," I said, "we've got a talent for doing the wrong thing. This is some kind of Top Secret military installation."

"Impossible," Foster replied. "This couldn't be a modern

structure, at the bottom of a rubble-filled shaft—"

"Let's get out of here, fast," I said. "We've probably set off an alarm already."

As if in answer, a low chime cut across our talk. Pearly light sprang up on a square panel, I got to my feet, moved over to stare at it. Foster came to my side.

"What do you make of it?" he said.

"I'm no expert on stone-age relics," I said. "But if that's not a radar screen, I'll eat it."

I sat down in the single chair before the dusty control console, and watched a red blip creep across the screen. Foster stood behind me.

"We owe a debt to that Ancient Sinner," he said. "Who would have dreamed he'd lead us here?"

"Ancient Sinner, Hell," I said. "This place is as modernistic as next year's juke box."

"Look at the symbols on the machines," Foster said. "They're identical with those in the first section of the Journal."

"All pot-hooks look alike to me," I said. "It's this screen that's got me worried. If I've got it doped out correctly, that blip is either a mighty slow airplane—or it's at one hell of an altitude."

"Modern aircraft operate at great heights," Foster said.

"Not at this height," I said. "Give me a few more minutes to study these scales…"

"There are a number of controls here," Foster said. "And it is more than obvious they are intended to activate mechanisms—"

"Don't touch 'em," I said. "Unless you want to start World War III."

"I hardly think the results would be so drastic," Foster said. "Surely this installation has a simple purpose, unconnected with modern wars—but very possibly connected with the mystery of the Journal—and of my own past."

THE less we know about this, the better," I said. "At least, if we don't mess with anything, we can always claim we just stepped in here to get out of the rain—"

"You're forgetting the Hunters," Foster said.

"Some new anti-personnel gimmick," I said.

"They came out of this shaft, Legion. It was opened by the pressure of the Hunters, bursting out."

"Why did they pick that precise moment—just as we arrived?" I asked.

"I think they were aroused," Foster said. "I think they sensed the presence of their ancient foe."

I swung around to look at him.

"I see the way your thoughts are running," I said. "You're their Ancient Foe, now, huh? Just let me get this straight: that means that umpteen hundred years ago, you personally, had a fight with the Hunters—here at Stonehenge. You killed a batch of them and ran. You hired some kind of Viking ship and crossed the Atlantic. Later on, you lost your memory, and started being a guy named Foster. A few weeks ago you lost it again. Is that the picture?"

"More or less."

"And now we're a couple of hundred feet under Stonehenge—after a brush with a crowd of luminous stinkbombs—and you're telling me you'll be nine hundred on your next birthday."

"Remember the entry in the journal, Legion? I came to the place of the Hunters, and it was a place I knew of old, and there was no hive, but a Pit built by men of the Two Worlds..."

"Okay," I said. "So you're pushing a thousand."

I glanced at the screen, got out a scrap of paper, and scribbled a rapid calculation. "Here's another big number for you. That object on the screen is at an altitude—give or take a few percent—of thirty thousand miles."

I TOSSED the pencil aside, swung around to frown at Foster. "What are we mixed up in, Foster? Not that I really want to know. I'm ready to go to a nice clean jail now, and pay my debt to society—"

"Calm down, Legion," Foster said. "You're raving."

"OK," I said, turning back to the screen. "You're the boss. Do what you like. It's just my reflexes wanting to run. I've got no place to run to. At least with you I've always got the wild hope that maybe you're not completely nuts, and that somehow—"

I sat upright, eyes on the screen. "Look at this, Foster," I snapped. A pattern of dots flashed across the screen, faded, flashed again...

"Some kind of IFF," I said. "A recognition signal. I wonder what we're supposed to do now."

Foster watched the screen, saying nothing.

"I don't like that thing blinking at us," I said. "It makes me feel conspicuous." I looked at the big red button beside the screen. "Maybe if I pushed that..." Without waiting to think it over, I jabbed at it.

A yellow light blinked on the control panel. On the screen, the pattern of dots vanished. The red blip separated, a smaller blip moving off at right angles to the main mass.

"I'm not sure you should have done that," Foster said.

"There is room for doubt," I said in a strained voice. "It looks like I've launched a bomb from the ship overhead."

THE climb back up the tunnel took three hours, and every foot of the way I was listening to a refrain in my head: This may be it; this may be it; this may be it...

I crawled out of the tunnel mouth and lay on my back, breathing hard. Foster groped his way out beside me.

"We'll have to get to the highway," I said, untying the ten-foot rope of ripped garments that had linked us during the climb. "There's a telephone at the pub; we'll notify the authorities..." I glanced up.

"Hold it," I said. I grabbed Foster's arm and pointed overhead. "What's that?"

Foster looked up. A brilliant point of blue light, brighter than a star, grew perceptibly as we watched.

"Maybe we won't get to notify anybody after all," I said. "I think that's our bomb—coming home to roost."

"That's illogical," Foster said. "The installation would hardly be arranged merely to destroy itself in so complex a manner."

"Let's get out of here," I yelled.

"It's approaching us very rapidly," Foster said. "The distance we could run in the next few minutes would be trivial by comparison with the killing radius of a modern bomb. We'll be safer sheltered in the cleft than in the open."

"We could slide back down the tunnel," I said.

"And be buried?"

"You're right; I'd rather fry on the surface."

We crouched, watching the blue glare directly overhead, growing larger, brighter. I could see Foster's face by its light now.

"That's no bomb," Foster said. "It's not falling; it's coming down slowly...like a—"

"Like a slowly falling bomb," I said. "And it's coming right down on top of us. Goodbye, Foster. I can't claim it's been fun knowing you, but it's been different. We'll feel the heat any second now. I hope it's fast."

The glaring disc was the size of the full moon now, unbearably bright. It lit the plain like a pale blue sun. There was no sound. As it dropped lower, the disc fore-shortened and I could see a dark shape above it, dimly lit by the glare thrown back from the ground.

"The thing is the size of a ferry boat," I said.

"It's going to miss us," Foster said. "It will come to ground to the east of us."

We watched the slender shape float down with dreamlike slowness, now five hundred feet above, now three hundred, then hovering just above the giant stones.

"It's coming down smack on top of Stonehenge," I yelled.

WE watched as the vessel settled into place dead center on the ancient ring of stones. For a moment they were vividly silhouetted against the flood of blue radiance; then abruptly, the glare faded and died.

"Foster," I said. "Do you think it's barely possible—"

A slit of yellow light appeared on the side of the hull, widened to a square. A ladder extended itself, dropping down to touch the ground.

"If somebody with tentacles starts down that ladder," I said, in an unnaturally shrill voice, "I'm getting out of here."

"No one will emerge," Foster said quietly. "I think we'll find, Legion, that this ship of space is at our disposal."

I'M not going aboard that thing," I said. "I'm not sure of much in this world, but I'm sure of that."

"Legion," Foster said, "this is no twentieth century military vessel. It obviously homed on the transmitter in the underground station, which appears to be directly under the old monument—which is several thousand years old—"

"And I'm supposed to believe the ship has been orbiting the Earth for the last few thousand years, waiting for someone to push the red button? You call that logical?"

"Given permanent materials—such as those the notebook

is made of—it's not impossible—or even difficult."

"We got out of the tunnel alive," I said. "Let's settle for that."

"We're on the verge of solving a mystery that goes back centuries," Foster said. "A mystery that I've pursued, if I understand the Journal, through many lifetimes—"

"One thing about losing your memory," I said. "You don't have any fixed ideas to get in the way of your theories."

Foster smiled grimly. "The trail has brought us here. I must follow it—wherever it leads."

I lay on the ground, staring up at the unbelievable shape, and the beckoning square of light. "This ship—or whatever it is," I said: "It drops down out of nowhere, and opens its doors—and you want to walk right into the cosy interior—"

"Listen!" Foster cut in.

I HEARD a low rumbling then, a sound that rolled ominously, like distant guns.

"More ships—" I started.

"Jet aircraft," Foster said. "From the bases in East Anglia probably. Of course, they'll have tracked our ship in—"

"That's all for me!" I yelled, getting to my feet. "The secret's out—"

"Get down, Legion," Foster shouted. The engines were a blanketing roar now.

"What for? They—"

Two long lines of fire traced themselves across the sky, curving down—

I hit the dirt behind the stone in the same instant the rockets struck. The shock wave slammed at the earth like a monster thunderclap, and I saw the tunnel mouth collapse. I twisted, saw the red interior of the jet tailpipe as the fighter hurtled past, rolling into a climbing turn.

"They're crazy," I yelled. "Firing on—"

A second barrage blasted across my indignation. I hugged the muck and waited while nine salvoes shook the earth. Then the rumble died, reluctantly. The air reeked of high explosives.

"We'd have been dead now if we'd tried the tunnel," I gasped, spitting dirt. "It caved at the first rocket. And if the ship was what you thought, Foster, they've destroyed something—"

The sentence died unnoticed. The dust was settling and through it the shape of the ship reared up, unchanged except that the square of light was gone. As I watched, the door opened again and the ladder ran out once more, invitingly.

"They'll try next time with atomics," I said. "That may be too much for the ship's defenses—and it will sure as hell be too much for us—"

"Listen," Foster cut in. A deeper rumble was building in the distance.

"To the ship!" Foster called. He was up and running, and I hesitated just long enough to think about trying for the highway and being caught in the open—and then I was running, too. Ahead, Foster stumbled crossing the ground that had been ripped up by the rocket bursts, made it to the ladder, and went up it fast. The growl of the approaching bombers grew, a snarl of deadly hatred. I leaped a still-smoking stone fragment, took the ladder in two jumps, plunged into the yellow-lit interior. Behind me, the door smacked shut.

I WAS standing in a luxuriously fitted circular room. There was a pedestal in the center of the floor, from which a polished bar projected. The bones of a man lay beside it. While I stared, Foster sprang forward, seized the bar, and pulled. It slid back easily. The lights flickered, and I had a moment of vertigo. Nothing else happened.

"Try it the other way," I yelled. "The bombs will fall any second—" I went for it, hand outstretched. Foster thrust in front of me. "Look!"

I stared at the glowing panel he was pointing to—a duplicate of the one in the underground chamber. It showed a curved white line, with a red point ascending from it.

"We're clear," Foster said. "We've made a successful takeoff."

"But we can't be moving—there's no acceleration. There must be sound-proofing—which is why we can't hear the noise of the bombers.

"No sound-proofing would help if we were at ground zero," Foster said. "This ship is the product of an advanced science. We've left the bombers far behind."

"Where are we going? Who's steering this thing?"

"It steers itself, I would judge," Foster said. "I don't know where we're going, but we're well on the way. There's no doubting that."

I looked at him in amazement. "You like this, don't you, Foster? You're having the time of your life."

"I can't deny that I'm delighted at this turn of events," Foster said. "Don't you see? This vessel is a launch, or lifeboat, under automatic control. And it's taking us to the mother ship."

"Okay, Foster," I said. "I'm with you." I looked at the skeleton on the floor behind him, and added; "But I sure hope we have better luck than the last passenger."

# CHAPTER SEVEN

IT was two hours later, and Foster and I stood silent before a ten-foot screen that had glowed into life when I touched a silver button beside it. It showed us a vast emptiness of bottomless black, set thick with coruscating points of polychrome brilliance that hurt to look at. And against that backdrop: a ship, vast beyond imagining, blotting out half the titanic vista with its bulk—

But dead.

Even from the distance of miles, I could sense it. The great black torpedo shape, dull moonlight glinting along the unbelievable length of its sleek flank, drifted: a derelict. I wondered for how many centuries it had waited here—and for what?

"I feel," said Foster, "somehow—I'm coming home."

I tried to say something, croaked, cleared my throat.

"If this is your jitney," I said, "I hope they didn't leave the meter ticking on you. We're broke."

"We're closing rapidly," said Foster. "Another ten minutes, I'd guess..."

"How do we go about heaving to, alongside? You didn't come across a book of instructions, did you?"

"I think I can predict that the approach will be automatic."

"This is your big moment, isn't it?" I said. "I've got to hand it to you, pal; you've won out by pluck."

The ship appeared to move smoothly closer, looming over

71

us, fine golden lines of decorative filigree work visible now against the black. A tiny square of pale light appeared, grew into a huge bay door that swallowed us.

The screen went dark, there was a gentle jar, then motionlessness. The port opened, silently.

"We've arrived," Foster said. "Shall we step out and have a look?"

"I wouldn't think of going back without one," I said. I followed him out and stopped dead gaping. I had expected an empty hold, bare metal walls. Instead, I found a vaulted cavern, shadowed, mysterious, rich with a thousand colors. There was a hint of strange perfume in the air, and I heard low music that muttered among stalagmite-like buttresses. There were pools, playing fountains, waterfalls, dim vistas stretching away, lit by slanting rays of muted sunlight.

"What kind of place is it?" I asked. "It's like a fairyland, or a dream."

"It's not an earthly scheme of decoration," Foster said, "but I find it strangely pleasing."

HEY, look over there," I yelped suddenly, pointing. An empty-eyed skull stared past me from the shadows at the base of a column.

Foster went over to the skull, stood looking down at it.

"There was a disaster here," he said. "That much is plain."

"It's creepy," I said. "Let's go back; I forgot to get film for my Brownie."

"The long-dead pose no threat," said Foster. He was kneeling, looking at the white bones. He picked up something, stared at it. "Look, Legion."

I went over. Foster held up a ring.

"We're onto something hot, pal," I said. "It's the twin to yours."

"I wonder...who he was."

I shook my head. "If we knew that—and who killed him —or what—"

"Let's go on. The answers must be here somewhere." Foster moved off toward a corridor that reminded me of a sunny avenue lined with chestnut trees—though there were no trees, and no sun. I followed, gaping.

For hours we wandered, looking, touching, not saying much but saturated in wonder, like kids in a toy factory. We came across another skeleton, lying among towering engines. Finally we paused in a giant storeroom stacked high with supplies.

"Have you stopped to think, Foster," I said, fingering a length of rose-violet cloth as thin as woven spider webs. "This boat's a treasure-house of marketable items. Talk about the wealth of the Indies—"

"I seek only one thing here, my friend," Foster said; "my past."

"Sure," I said. "But just in case you don't find it, you might consider the business angle. We can set up a regular shuttle run, hauling stuff down—"

"You Earthmen," sighed Foster. "For you, every new experience is immediately assessed in terms of its merchandising possibilities. Well, I leave that to you."

"Okay okay," I said. "You go on ahead and scout around down that way, if you want—where the technical-looking stuff is. I want to browse around here for a while."

"As you wish."

"We'll meet at this end of the big hall we passed back there. Okay?"

Foster nodded and went on. I turned to a bin filled with what looked like unset emeralds the size of walnuts. I picked up a handful, juggled them lovingly.

"Anyone for marbles?" I murmured to myself.

HOURS later I came along a corridor that was like a path through a garden that was a forest, crossed a ballroom like a meadow floored in fine-grained rust-red wood and shaded by giant ferns, and went under an arch into the hall where Foster sat at a long table cut from yellow marble. A light the color of sunrise gleamed through tall pseudo-windows.

I dumped an armful of books on the table. "Look at these," I said. "All made from the same stuff as the Journal. And the pictures..."

I flipped open one of the books, a heavy folio-sized volume, to a double-page spread in color showing a group of bearded Arabs in dingy white djellabas staring toward the camera, a flock of thin goats in the background. It looked like the kind of picture the National Geographic runs, except that the quality of the color and detail was equal to the best color transparencies.

"I can't read the print," I said, "but I'm a whiz at looking at pictures. Most of the books show scenes like I hope I never see in the flesh, but I found a few that were made on Earth—God knows how long ago."

"Travel books, perhaps," Foster said.

"Travel books that you could sell to any university on Earth for their next year's budget. Take a look at this one."

Foster looked across at the panoramic shot of a procession of shaven-headed men in white sarongs, carrying a miniature golden boat on their shoulders, descending a long flight of white stone steps leading from a colonnade of heroic human figures with folded arms and painted faces. In the background, brick-red cliffs loomed up, baked in desert heat.

"That's the temple of Hat-Shepsut in its prime," I said. "Which makes this print close to four thousand years old. Here's another I recognize." I turned to a smaller, aerial view, showing a gigantic pyramid, its polished stone facing chipped in places and with a few panels missing from the lower levels revealing the cruder structure of massive blocks beneath.

"That's one of the major pyramids, maybe Khufu's," I said. "It was already a couple thousand years old, and falling into disrepair. And look at this—" I opened another volume, showed Foster a vivid photograph of a great shaggy elephant with a pinkish trunk upraised between wide-curving yellow tusks.

"A mastodon," I said. "And there's a woolly rhino, and an ugly-looking critter that must be a sabre-tooth. This book is old…"

"A lifetime of rummaging wouldn't exhaust the treasures aboard this ship," said Foster.

"How about bones? Did you find any more?"

Foster nodded. "There was a disaster of some sort. Perhaps disease. None of the bones was broken."

I CAN'T figure the one in the lifeboat," I said. "Why was he wearing a necklace of bear's teeth?" I sat down across from Foster. "We've got plenty of mysteries to solve, all right, but there are some other items we'd better talk about. For instance: where's the kitchen? I'm getting hungry."

Foster handed me a black rod from among several that lay on the table. "I think this may be important," he said.

"What is it? a chop stick?"

"Touch it to your head, above the ear."

"What does it do—give you a massage?" I pressed it to my temple…

*I was in a grey-walled room, facing a towering surface of ribbed metal. I reached out, placed my hands over the proper perforations. The housings opened. For apparent malfunction in the quaternary field amplifiers, I knew, auto-inspection circuit override was necessary before activation—*

I blinked, looked around at the rod in my hand.

"I was in some kind of powerhouse," I said. "There was something wrong with—with…"

"The Quaternary field amplifiers," Foster said.

"I seemed to be right there," I said. "I understood exactly what it was all about."

"These are technical manuals," Foster said. "They'll tell us everything we need to know about the ship."

"I was thinking about what I was getting ready to do," I said, "the way you do when you're starting into a job; I was trouble-shooting the Quaternary whatzits—and I knew how…"

Foster got to his feet and moved toward the doorway. "We'll have to start at one end of the library and work our way through," he said. "It will take us awhile, but we'll get the facts we need. Then we can plan."

FOSTER picked a handful of briefing rods from the racks in the comfortably furnished library and started in. The first thing we needed was a clue as to where to look for food and beds, or for operating instructions for the ship itself. I hoped we might find the equivalent of a library card-catalog; then we could put our hands on what we wanted in a hurry.

I went to the far end of the first rack and spotted a short row of red rods that stood out vividly among the black ones. I took one out, thought it over, decided it was unlikely that it was any more dangerous than the others, and put it against my temple…

*As the bells rang, I applied neuro-vascular tension, suppressed cortical areas upsilon-zeta and iota, and stood by for—*

I jerked the rod from my head, my ears still ringing with the shrill alarm. The effect of the rods was like reality itself, but intensified, all attention focussed single-mindedly on the experience at hand. I thought of the entertainment potentialities of the idea. You could kill a tiger, ride an airplane down in flames, face the heavyweight champion— I wondered about the stronger sensations, like pain and fear. Would they seem as real as the impulse to check the whatchamacallits or tighten up your cortical thingamajigs?

I tried another rod.

*At the sound of the apextone, I racked instruments, walked, not ran, to the nearest transfer-channel—*

Another:

*Having assumed duty as Alert Officer, I reported first to coordination Control via short-line, and confirmed rapport—*

These were routine SOP's covering simple situations aboard ship. I skipped a few, tried again:

*Needing a xivometer, I keyed instruction-complex One, followed with the code—*

THREE rods further along, I got this:

*The situation falling outside my area of primary conditioning, I reported in corpo to Technical Briefing, Level Nine, Section Four, Subsection Twelve, Preliminary. I recalled that it was now necessary to supply my activity code...my activity code...my activity code...(A sensation of disorientation grew; confused images flickered like vague background-noise; then a clear voice cut in:)*

YOU HAVE SUFFERED PARTIAL PERSONALITY-- FADE. DO NOT BE ALARMED. SELECT A GENERAL BACKGROUND ORIENTATION ROD FROM THE NEAREST EMERGENCY RACK. ITS LOCATION IS...

*I was moving along the stacks, to pause in front of a niche where a U-shaped plastic strip was clamped to the wall. I removed it, fitted it to my head—*

*(Then:) I was moving along the stacks, to pause in front of a niche*

—

I was leaning against the wall, my head humming. The red stick lay on the floor at my feet. That last bit had been potent: something about a, general background briefing—

"Hey, Foster!" I called, "I think I've got something...!'

"As I see it," I said, "this background briefing should tell us all we need to know about the ship; then we can plan our next move more intelligently. We'll know what we're doing!" I took the thing from the wall, just as I had seemed to do in the phantom scene the red rod had projected for me.

"These things make me dizzy," I said, handing it to Foster. "Anyway, you're the logical one to try it."

He took the plastic shape, went to the reclining seat at the near end of the library hall, and settled himself. "I have an idea this one will hit harder than the others," he said.

He fitted the clamp to his head and...instantly his eyes glazed; he slumped back, limp.

"Foster!" I yelled. I jumped forward, started to pull the plastic piece from his head, then hesitated. Maybe Foster's abrupt reaction was standard procedure. In any case whatever harm this gadget could do to Foster's brain had already been done. I might as well let the process take its course. But I didn't like it much.

I went on reasoning with myself. After all, this was what the red rod had indicated as normal procedure in a given emergency. Foster was merely having his faded personality touched up. And his full-blown, three-dimensional personality was what we needed to give us the answers to a lot of the questions we'd been asking. Though the ship and everything in it had lain unused and silent for forgotten millenia, still the library should be good. The librarian was gone from his post these thirty centuries, and Foster was lying unconscious, and I was thirty thousand miles from home—but I shouldn't let trifles like that worry me...

I GOT up and prowled the room. There wasn't much to look at except stacks and more stacks. The knowledge stored here was fantastic, both in magnitude and character. If I ever got home with a load of these rods...

I strolled through a door leading to another room. It was small, functional, dimly lit. The middle of the room was occupied by a large and elaborate divan with a cap-shaped fitting at one end. Other curious accoutrements were ranked along the walls. There wasn't much in them to thrill me. But bonewise I had hit the jackpot.

Two skeletons lay near the door, in the final slump of death. Another lay beside the fancy couch. There was a long-bladed dagger beside it.

I squatted beside the two near the door and examined them closely. As far as I could tell, they were as human as I was. I wondered what kind of men they had been, what kind of world they had come from, that could build a ship like this and stock it as it was stocked.

The dagger that lay near the other bones was interesting: it seemed to be made of a transparent orange metal, and its hilt was stamped in a repeated pattern of the Two Worlds motif. It was the first clue as to what had taken place among these men when they last lived: not a complete clue, but a start.

I took a closer look at an apparatus like a dentist's chair parked against the wall. There were spidery-looking metal arms mounted above it, and a series of colored glass lenses. A row of dull silver cylinders was racked against the wall. Another projected from a socket at the side of the machine. I took it out and looked at it. It was of plain pewter-colored plastic, heavy and smooth. I felt pretty sure it was a close cousin to the chop sticks stored in the library. I wondered what brand of information was recorded in it as I dropped it in my pocket.

I lit a cigarette and went back out to where Foster lay. He was still in the same position as when I had left him. I sat down on the floor beside the couch to wait. It was an hour before he stirred. He reached up, pulled off the plastic head-piece, dropped it on the floor.

"Are you okay?" I asked.

Foster looked at me, his eyes travelling up to my uncombed hair and down to my scuffed shoes. His eyes narrowed in a faint frown. Then he said something—in a language that seemed to be all Z's and Q's.

"Enough surprises, Foster," I said hoarsely. "Talk American."

He stared into my eyes, then glanced around the room.

"This is a ship's library," he said.

I heaved a sigh of relief. Foster was watching my face. "What was it all about?" I said. "What have you found out?"

"I know you," said Foster slowly. "Your name is Legion."

I nodded. I could feel myself getting tense again. "Sure, you know me." I put a hand on his shoulder. "You remember: we were—"

He shook my hand oft. "That is not the custom in Vallon," he said coldly.

"Vallon?" I echoed. "What kind of routine is this, Foster?"

"Where are the others?"

"There's a couple of 'others' in the next room," I snapped. "But they've lost a lot of weight. Outside of them there's only me—"

Foster looked at me as if I wasn't there. "I remember Vallon," he said. He put a hand to his head. "But I remember too a barbaric world, brutal and primitive. You were there. We traveled in a crude rail-car, and then in a barge that wallowed in the sea. There were narrow, ugly rooms, evil odors, harsh noises...and The Hunters! We fled from them, Legion, you and I. And I remember a landing-ring..." He paused. "Strange, it had lost its cap-stones and fallen into ruin."

"Us natives call it Stonehenge."

"The Hunters burst out of the earth. We fought them. But why should the Hunters seek me?"

"I was hoping you'd tell me," I said. "Do you know where this ship came from? And why?"

"This is a ship of the Two Worlds," he replied. "But I know nothing of how it came to be here."

"How about all that stuff in the journal? Maybe now you —"

"The journal!" Foster broke in. "Where is it?"

"In your coat pocket, I guess."

Foster felt through his jacket awkwardly, brought out the journal. He opened it and looked at the part written in the curious alien characters that nobody had been able to decipher.

But he was reading it.

FOR hours I had waited while Foster read. At last he leaned back in his chair and sighed.

"My name," he said, "was Qulqlan. And this," he laid his hand upon the book, "is my story. This is one part of the past I was seeking. And I remember none of it..."

"Tell me what the journal says."

Foster picked it up. "It seems that I awoke once before, in a small room aboard this vessel. I was lying on a memo-couch, by which circumstance I knew that I had suffered a Change—"

"You mean you'd lost your memory?"

"And regained it—on the couch. My memory-trace had been re-impressed on my mind. I awoke knowing my identity, but not how I came to be aboard this vessel. The journal says that my last memory was of a building beside the Shallow Sea."

"Where's that?

"On a far world—called Vallon."

"Yeah? And what next?"

"I looked around me and saw four men lying on the floor, slashed and bloody. One was alive. I gave him what emergency treatment I could, then searched the ship. I found three more men, dead; none living. Then the Hunters attacked, swarming to me. They would have sucked the life from me—and I had no shield of light. I fled to the lifeboat, carrying the wounded man. I descended to the planet below: your Earth. The man died there. He had been my friend, a man named Ammaerln. I buried him in a shallow depression in the earth and marked the place with a stone."

"The Ancient Sinner," I said.

"Yes...I suppose it was his bones the lay brother found."

"And we found out last night that the depression was the result of dirt sifting down into the ventilator shaft. But I guess you didn't know anything about the underground installation, way back then. Doesn't the journal say anything...?"

"No, there is no mention made of it here."

"How about the Hunters? How did they get to Earth?"

"They are insubstantial creatures," said Foster, "yet they can endure the vacuum of space. I can only surmise that they followed the lifeboat down."

"They were tailing you?"

"Yes; but I have no idea why they pursued me. They're harmless creatures in the natural state, used to seek out the rare fugitive from justice on Vallon. They can be attuned to the individual; thereafter, they follow him and mark him out for capture."

"Say, what were you: a big time racketeer on Vallon?"

"THE journal is frustratingly silent as to my Vallonian

career," said Foster. "But this whole matter of the unexplained inter-galactic voyage and the evidence of violence aboard the ship make me wonder whether I was being exiled for crimes done in the Two Worlds."

"So they sicked the Hunters on you?" I said. "But why did they hang around at Stonehenge all this time?"

"There was a trickle of power feeding the screens," said Foster. "They need a source of electrical energy to live; until a hundred years ago it was the only one on the planet."

"How did they get down into the shaft without opening it up?"

"Given time, they pass easily through porous substances. But, of course, last night, when I came on them after their long fast, they simply burst through in their haste."

"Okay. What happened next? –after you buried the man."

"The journal tells that I was set upon by natives, men who wore the hides of animals. One of their number entered the ship. He must have moved the drive lever. It lifted, leaving me marooned."

"So those were his bones we found in the boat," I mused: "the ones with the bear's-tooth necklace. I wonder why he didn't come into the ship."

"Undoubtedly he did. But remember the skeleton we found just inside the landing port? That must have been a fairly fresh and rather gory corpse at the time the savage stepped aboard. It probably seemed to him all too clear an indication of what lay in store for himself if he ventured further. In his terror he must have retreated to the boat to wait, and there starved to death.

"He was stranded in your world, and you were stranded in his."

"Yes," said Foster. "And then, it seems, I lived among the brutemen and came to be their king. I waited there by the landing-ring through many years in the hope of rescue. Because I did not age as the natives did, I was worshipped as a god. I would have built a signaling device, but there were no pure metals, nothing I could use. I tried to teach them, but it was a work of centuries."

"But how could one go on living—for hundreds of years? Are you people supermen that live forever?"

"Not forever. But the natural span of a human life is very great. Among your people, there is a wasting disease from which you all die young."

"That's no disease," I said. "You just naturally get old and die."

"The human mind is a magnificent instrument," Foster said; "not meant to wither quickly."

"Why didn't you catch this 'disease'?"

"All Vallonians are inoculated against it."

FOSTER turned back to the Journal. "I ruled many peoples under many names," he said. "I traveled in many lands, seeking for skilled metal-workers, glass-blowers, wise men. But always I returned to the landing-ring."

"It must have been tough," I said, "exiled on a strange world, living out your life in a wilderness, century after century…"

"My life was not without interest," Foster said. "I watched my savage people put aside their animal hides and learn the ways of civilization. I built a great city, and I tried—foolishly—to teach their noble caste the code of chivalry of the two Worlds. But although they sat at a round table like the great Ringboard at Okk-Hamiloth, they never really understood. And then they grew too wise, and wondered at their king who never aged. I left them, and tried again to, build a long-signaler. The Hunters sensed it, and swarmed to me. I drove them off with fires, and then I grew curious, and followed them back to their nest—"

"I know," I said. " 'And it was a place you knew of old; no hive but a Pit built by men'."

"They overwhelmed me; I barely escaped with my life. Starvation had made the Hunters vicious. They would have drained my body of its life-energy."

"And if you'd known the transmitter was there—but you didn't. So you put an ocean between you and them."

"They found me even there. Each time I destroyed many of them, and fled. But always a few lived to breed and seek me out again."

"Didn't your signaler work?"

"No. It was a hopeless attempt. Only a highly developed technology could supply the raw materials. I could only teach what I knew, encourage the development of the sciences, and wait. And then I began to forget."

"Why?"

"A mind grows weary," Foster said. "It is the price of longevity. It must renew itself. Shock and privation hasten the change. I had held it off for many centuries. Now I felt it coming on me.

"At home, on Vallon, a man would record his memory at such a time, store it electronically in a recording device, and, after the Change, use the memory-trace to restore, in his renewed body, his old recollections in toto. But, marooned as I was, my memories, once lost, were gone forever.

"I did what I could: I prepared a safe place, and wrote messages that I would find when I awoke—"

"When you woke up in the hotel," I said, "you were young again, overnight. How could it happen?"

"When the mind renews itself, erasing the scars of the years, the body, too, regenerates."

WHEN I first met you," I said, "you told me about

waking up back in 1918, with no memory."

"Yours is a harsh world, Legion. I must have forgotten, many times. Somewhere, sometime, I lost the vital link, forgot my quest; when the Hunters came again, I fled, not understanding."

There was a silence, then Foster spoke in a faraway voice.

"What came to pass aboard this ship all those centuries ago?" he said. "Why was I here? And what killed the others? Someday, somehow I must learn the truth of this matter."

"What I can't figure out is why somebody didn't come after this ship. It was right here in orbit."

"Consider the immensity of space, Legion. This is one tiny world, among the stars."

"But there was a station here, fitted out for handling your ships. That sounds like it was a regular port of call. And the books with the pictures: they prove your people have been here off and on for thousands of years. Why would they stop coming?"

"There are such beacons on a thousand worlds," said Foster. "Think of it as a buoy marking a reef, a trailblaze in the wilderness. Ages could pass before a wanderer chanced this way again. The fact that the ventilator shaft at Stonehenge was choked with the debris of centuries when I first landed there shows how seldom this world was visited."

I thought about it. Trying to piece together Foster's past would be a slow process. I had an idea:

"Say, you said you were in the memory machine. You woke up there—and you'd just had your memory restored. Why not do the same thing again, now? That is, if your brain can take another pounding this soon."

"Yes," he said. He stood up abruptly. "There's just a chance. Come on!"

I FOLLOWED him out of the library into the room with

the bones.

Foster walked across to the fancy couch, leaned down, then shook his head. "No," he said. "Of course it wouldn't be here..."

"What?"

"My memory-trace: the one that was used to restore my memory—that other time."

Suddenly I recalled the cylinder I had pocketed hours before. With a surprising flutter at my heart I held it up. "This it?"

Foster glanced at it briefly. "No, that's an empty—like those you see filed over there." He pointed to the rack of pewter-colored cylinders on the opposite wall. "They would be used for emergency recordings. Regular multi-life memory-traces would be key-coded with a pattern of colored lines."

"It figures," I said. "That would have been too easy."

"It doesn't matter, really. When I return to Vallon, I'll recover my past. There are vaults in Okk-Hamiloth where every citizen's trace is stored."

"I guess you'll be eager to get back there," I said. "Have you been able to figure out how long you were marooned down on Earth!"

"Since I descended from this ship, Legion," he said, "three thousand years have passed."

"I'm going to miss you, Foster," I said. "You know, I was kind of getting used to being an apprentice nut."

"Come with me to Vallon, Legion," he said.

"Thanks anyway, buddy," I said. "I'd like to see those other worlds of yours but in the end I'd regret it. I'd just sit around on Vallon pining for home: beat-up people, and all."

"THEN what can I do for you, Legion, to reward your loyalty and express my gratitude!"

"Let me take the lifeboat, and stock it with a few goodies from the library, and some of those marbles from the storeroom, and a couple of the smaller mechanical gadgets. I think I know how to merchandise them in a way that'll leave the economy on an even keel—and incidentally set me up for life. As you said, I'm a materialist."

"Take whatever you desire."

"One thing I'll have to do when I get back," I said, "is open the tunnel at Stonehenge enough to sneak a thermite bomb down it—if they haven't already found the beacon station."

"As I judge the temper of the local people," Foster said, "the secret is safe for at least three generations."

"I'll bring the boat down in a blind spot where radar won't pick it up," I said. "Our timing was good; in another few years, it wouldn't have been possible."

"And this ship would soon have been discovered."

I looked at the great smooth sphere hanging, haloed, against utter black. The Pacific Ocean threw back a brilliant image of the sun.

I turned to Foster. "We're in a ten-hour orbit," I said. "We'd better get moving. I want to put the boat down in southern South America. I know a place there where I can unload without answering too many questions."

"You have several hours before the most favorable launch time," Foster said. "There's no hurry."

"Maybe not, but I've got a lot to do—and I'm eager to start."

# CHAPTER EIGHT

I SAT on the terrace watching the sun go down into the sea and thinking about Foster, somewhere out there beyond the purple palaces on the far horizon, in the ship that had waited for him for three thousand years, heading home at last. It was strange to reflect that for him, travelling near the speed of light, only a few weeks had passed, while three years went by for me—three fast years that I had put to good use.

The toughest part had been the first few months, after I put the lifeboat down in a canyon in the desert country south of a little town called Itzenca, in Peru. I hiked to town, carrying a pack with a few carefully selected items to start my new career. It took me two weeks to work, lie, barter, and plead my way to the seaport town of Callao and another week to line up passage home as a deck hand on a banana scow. I disappeared over the side at Tampa, and made it to Miami without attracting attention. As far as I could tell, the cops had already lost interest in me.

The items I had brought with me from the lifeboat were a pocketful of little grey dominoes that were actually movie film, and a small projector to go with them. I didn't offer them for sale, direct. I made arrangements with an old acquaintance in the business of making pictures with low costume budgets for private showings; I set up the apparatus and projected my films, and he copied them in 35 mm. I told him that I'd smuggled them in from East Germany.

I had twelve pictures altogether; with a little judicious cutting and a dubbed-in commentary, they made up into fast-moving twenty-minute short subjects. He got in touch with a friend in the distribution end in New York, and after a little cagy fencing over contract terms, we agreed on a deal that paid me a hundred thousand for the twelve, with an option on another dozen at the same price.

Within a week after the pictures hit the neighborhood theatres around Bayonne, New Jersey, in a cautious try-out, I had offers up to half a million for my next consignment, no questions asked. I left my pal Mickey to handle the details, on a percentage basis, and headed back for Itzenca.

THE lifeboat was just as I'd left it; it would have been all right for another fifty years, as far as the danger of anybody stumbling over it was concerned. I explained to the crew I brought out with me that it was a fake rocket ship, a prop I was using for a film I was making. They went to work setting up a system of camouflage nets (part of the plot, I told them) and unloading my cargo.

A year after my homecoming, I had my island—a square mile of perfect climate, fifteen miles off the Peruvian coast—and a house that was tailored to my every whim. The uppermost floor—almost a tower—was a strong-room, and it was there that I had stored my stock in trade. I had sold the best of the hundred or so films I had picked out before leaving Foster, but there were plenty of other items. The projector itself was the big prize. The self-contained power unit converted nuclear energy to light with 99 percent efficiency. It scanned the 'films', one molecular layer at a time, and projected a continuous picture. The color and sound were absolutely lifelike.

The principles involved in the projector were new, and—

in theory, at least—way over the heads of our local physicists. But the practical application was nothing much. I figured that, with the right contacts in scientific circles to help me introduce the system, I had a billion-dollar industry up my sleeve. I had already fed a few little gimmicks into the market; a tough paper, suitable for shirts and underwear; a chemical that bleached teeth white as the driven snow; an all-color pigment for artists. With the knowledge I had absorbed from all the briefing rods I had studied, I had the techniques of a hundred new industries at my fingertips—and I hadn't exhausted the possibilities yet.

I spent most of a year roaming the world, discovering all the things that a free hand with a dollar bill could do for a man. Then followed a year of fixing up the island.

NOW, after the first big thrill of economic freedom had worn off, it was beginning to get me: boredom, the disease of the idle rich that I had sworn would never touch me. But thinking about wealth and having it on your hands are two different things, and I was beginning to remember almost with nostalgia, the tough old times when every day was an adventure, full of cops and missed meals and a thousand unappeased desires.

I finished up my expensive cigar and leaned forward to drop it in a big silver ashtray, when something caught my eye out across the red-painted water. I sat squinting at it, then went inside and came out with a pair of 12 x binoculars. I focussed them and studied the dark speck that stood out clearly now against the gaudy sky. It was a heavy looking power boat, heading dead toward my island.

I watched it come closer, and ease alongside the hundred foot concrete jetty I had built below the sea wall. The engines died, and the boat sat, in a sudden silence. Two heavy deck guns were mounted on the foredeck, and there were four torpedoes slung in launching cradles. I saw ranks of helmeted men drawn up on deck. They shuffled off onto the pier, formed up into two squads. I counted; forty-eight men, and a couple of officers. There was the faint sound of orders being barked, and the column stepped off, moving along the paved road that led up to the house. They halted. The two officers, wearing class A's, and a tubby civilian with a brief case approached the steps leading up to my perch.

THE leading officer, a brigadier general, no less, looked up at me.

"I am General Smale," he said. "This is Colonel Sanchez of the Peruvian Army—" he indicated the other military type —"and Mr. Pruffy of the American Embassy at Lima."

I nodded.

"We would like to talk with you about an official matter, Mr. Legion. It's of great importance, involving the security of your country."

"OK, General," I said. "Come on up."

They filed onto the terrace, hesitated, then shook hands, and sat down in the empty chairs. Pruffy held his briefcase in his lap.

"I'm here," the general said, "to ask you a few questions, Mr. Legion. Mr. Pruffy represents the Department of State in the matter, and Colonel Sanchez—"

"Don't tell me," I said. "He represents the Peruvian government, which is why I don't ask you what the hell an armed American force is doing wandering around on Peruvian soil. What's it all about, Smale?"

"I'll come directly to the point," he said. "For some time, the investigative and security agencies of the US government have been building a file on what for lack of a better name has been called 'The Martians'. A little over three years ago an unidentified flying object appeared on a number of radar screens, descending from extreme altitude. It came to earth at..." he hesitated.

"Don't tell me you came all the way out here to tell me you can't tell me," I said.

"—a site in England," Smale said. "American aircraft were dispatched to investigate the object. Before they could make identification, it rose again, accelerated at tremendous speed, and was lost at an altitude of several hundred miles."

"I thought we had better radar than that," I said. "The satellite program—"

"No such specialized equipment was available," Smale said. "An intensive investigation turned up the fact that two strangers—possibly Americans—had visited the site only a few hours before the—ah—visitation."

I nodded. I was thinking about the close call I'd had when I went back to see about putting a bomb down the shaft to obliterate the beacon station. There were plainclothes men all over the place, like old maids at a movie star's funeral. It was just as well; they never found it. The rocket blasts had collapsed the tunnel, and apparently the whole underground installation was made of nonmetallic substances that didn't show up on detecting equipment. I had an idea metal was passe where Foster came from.

SOME months later," Smale went on, "a series of rather curious short films went on exhibition in the United States. They showed scenes representing conditions on other planets, as well as ancient and prehistoric incidents here on Earth. They were prefaced with explanations that they merely represented the opinions of science as to what was likely to be found on distant worlds. They attracted wide interest, and with few exceptions, scientists praised their verisimilitude."

"I admire a clever fake," I said. "With a topical subject

like space travel—"

"One item which was commented on as a surprising inaccuracy, in view of the technical excellence of the other films," Smale said, "was the view of our planet from space, showing the Earth against a backdrop of stars. A study of the constellations by astronomers quickly indicated a 'date' of approximately 7000 B. C. for the scene. Oddly, the north polar cap was shown centered on Hudson's Bay. No South Polar cap was in evidence. The continent of Antarctica appeared to be at a latitude of some 30°, entirely free of ice."

I looked at him and waited.

"Now, studies made since that time indicate that nine thousand years ago, the North Pole was indeed centered on Hudson's Bay," Smale said. "And Antarctica was in fact ice-free."

"That idea's been around a long time," I said. "There was, a theory—"

"Then there was the matter of the views of Mars," the general said. "The aerial shots of the 'canals' were regarded as very cleverly done." He turned to Pruffy, who opened his briefcase and handed a couple of photos across.

"This is a scene taken from the film," Smale said.

It was an 8x10 color shot, showing a row of mounds drifted with pinkish dust, against a blue-black horizon. Smale placed another photo beside the first.

"This one," he said, "was taken by automatic cameras in the successful Mars probe of last year."

I looked. The second shot was fuzzy, and the color was shifted badly toward the blue, but there was no mistaking the scene. The mounds were drifted a little deeper, and the angle was different, but they were the same mounds.

"In the meantime," Smale bored on relentlessly, "a number of novel products appeared on the market. Chemists and physicists alike were dumfounded at the theoretical base implied by the techniques involved. One of the products—a type of pigment—embodied a completely new concept in crystallography."

"Progress," I said. "Why, when I was a boy—"

"It was an extremely tortuous trail we followed," Smale said. "But we found that all these curious observations making up the 'Martians' file had only one factor in common —you, Mr. Legion."

## CHAPTER NINE

IT was a few minutes after sunrise, and Smale and I were back on the terrace toying with the remains of ham steaks and honeydew.

"Beer for breakfast," I said. "A little unusual, maybe, but it goes swell with ham and eggs. That's one advantage of being in jail in your own house—the food's good."

"I can understand your feelings," Smale said. "It was my hope that you'd see fit to co-operate voluntarily."

"Take your army and sail off into the sunrise, General," I said. "Then maybe I'll be in a position to do something voluntary."

"Your patriotism alone—"

"My patriotism keeps telling me that where I come from a citizen has certain legal rights," I said.

"This is a matter that transcends legal technicalities," Smale said. "I'll tell you quite frankly, the presence of the task force here only received ex post facto approval by the

Peruvian government. They were faced with the *fait accompli*. I mention this only to indicate just how strongly the government feels in this matter."

"Seeing you hit the beach with a platoon of infantry was enough of a hint for me," I said. "You're lucky I didn't wipe you out with my disintegrator rays."

Smale choked on a bit of melon.

"Just kidding," I said. "But I haven't given you any trouble. Why the reinforcements?"

Smale stared at me. "What reinforcements?"

I pointed with a fork. He turned, gazed out to sea. A conning tower was breaking the surface, leaving a white wake behind. It rose higher, water streaming off the deck. A hatch popped open, and men poured out, lining up. Smale got to his feet, his napkin falling to the floor.

"Sergeant!" he yelled. I sat, open-mouthed, as Smale jumped to the stair, went down it three steps at a time. I heard him bellowing, the shouts of men and the clatter of rifles being unstacked, feet pounding. The Marines were forming up on the lawn.

Smale bounded back up the stairs. "You're my prime responsibility, Legion," he barked. "I want you in the cellar for maximum security."

"What's this all about?" I asked. "Interservice rivalry? You afraid the sailors are going to steal the glory?"

"That's a nuclear-powered sub," Smale barked. "Gagarin class; it belongs to the Soviet Navy."

I STOOD there with my mouth open trying hard to think fast. I hadn't been too startled when the Marines showed up; I had gone over the legal aspects of my situation months before, with a platoon of high-priced legal talent; I knew that sooner or later somebody would come around to hit me for tax evasion, draft dodging, or overtime parking; but I was in the clear. The government might resent my knowing a lot of things it didn't, but no one could ever prove I'd swiped them from Uncle Sam. In the end, they'd have to let me go—and my account in a Swiss bank would last me, even if they managed to suppress any new developments from my fabulous lab. In a way, I was glad the show-down had come.

But I'd forgotten about the Russians. Naturally, they'd be interested, and their spies were at least as good as the intrepid agents of the US Secret Service. I should have realized that sooner or later, they'd pay a call—and the legal niceties wouldn't slow them down. They'd slap me into a brain laundry, and sweat every last secret out of me as casually as I'd squeeze a lemon.

The sub was fully surfaced now, and I was looking down the barrels of half a dozen five-inch rifles, anyone of which could blast Smale's navy out of the water with one salvo. There were a couple of hundred men, I estimated, putting landing boats over the side and spilling into them. Down on the lawn, the sergeant was snapping orders, and the men were double-timing off to positions that must have been spotted in advance. It looked like the Russians weren't entirely unexpected. This was a game the big boys were playing, and I was just a pawn, caught in the middle. My rose picture of me confounding the bureaucrats was fading fast. My island was about to become a battlefield, and whichever way it turned out, I'd be the loser. I had one slim possibility; to get lost in the shuffle.

"Sorry, General," I said and slammed a hard right to his stomach and a left to the jaw. He dropped. I jumped over him, plunged through the french doors, and took the spiral glass stairway four at a time, whirled, and slammed the strong-room door behind me. The armored walls would stand anything short of a direct hit with a good sized artillery shell, and the boys down below were unlikely to use any heavy stuff for fear of damaging the goods they'd been sent out to collect. I was safe for a little while.

NOW I had to do some fast, accurate thinking. I couldn't carry much with me—when and if I made it off the island. A few briefing rods, maybe; what was left of the movies.

I rummaged through odds and ends, stuffing small items into my pockets. I came across a dull silvery cylinder, three inches long, striped in black and gold—a memory trace. It reminded me of something...

That was an idea. I still had the U-shaped plastic headpiece that Foster had used to acquire a background knowledge of his old home-world. I had tried it once—for a moment. It had given me a headache in two seconds flat, just pressed against my temple. It had been lying here ever since. But maybe now was the time to try it again. Half the items I had here in my strong-room were mysteries, like the silver cylinder in my hand, but I knew exactly what the plastic headband could give me. It contained all anyone needed to know about Vallon and the Two Worlds, and all the marvels they possessed.

I glanced out the armor-glass window. Smale's Marines were trotting across the lawn; the Russians were fanning out along the water's edge. It looked like business all right. It would take them a while to get warmed up—and more time still to decide to blast me out of my fort. It had taken an hour or so for Foster to soak up the briefing; maybe I wouldn't be much longer at it.

I tossed the cylinder aside, tried a couple of drawers, found the inconspicuous strip of plastic that encompassed a whole civilization. I carried it across to a chair, settled myself, then hesitated. This thing had been designed for an alien brain. Suppose it burnt out my wiring, left me here gibbering, for Smale or the Russkis to work over? But the alternative was to leave my island virtually empty-handed.

No, I wouldn't go back to poverty without a struggle. What I could carry in my head would give me independence —even immunity from the greed of nations. I could barter my knowledge for my freedom.

There were plenty of things wrong with the picture, but it was the best I could do on short notice. Gingerly I fitted the U-shaped band to my head. There was a feeling of pressure, then a sensation like warm water rising about me. Panic tried to rise, faded. A voice seemed to reassure me. I was among friends, I was safe, all was well...

## CHAPTER TEN

I LAY in the dark, the memory of towers and trumpets and fountains of fire in my mind. I put up my hand, felt a coarse garment. Had I but dreamed...? I stirred. Light blazed in a widening band above my face. Through narrowed eyes I saw a room, a mean chamber, dusty, littered with ill-assorted rubbish. In a wall there was a window. I went to it, stared out upon a green sward, a path that curved downward to a white strand. It was a strange scene, and yet—

A wave of vertigo swept over me, faded. I tried to remember.

I reached up, felt something clamped over my head. I pulled it off and it fell to the floor with a faint clatter: a broad-spectrum briefing device, of the type used to indoctrinate unidentified citizens who had undergone a

Change unprepared...

Suddenly, like water pouring down a drain, the picture in my mind faded, left me standing in my old familiar junk room, with a humming in my head and a throb in my temples. I had been about to try the briefing gimmick, and had wondered if it would work. It had—with a vengeance. For a minute there I had stumbled around the room like a stranger, yearning for dear old Vallon. I could remember the feeling—but it was gone now. I was just me, in trouble as usual.

A rattle of gunfire outside brought me to the window in a jump. It was the same view as a few moments before, but it made more sense now. There was the still-smoking wreckage of the PT boat, sunk in ten feet of water a few yards from the end of the jetty. Somebody must have tried to make a run for it. The Russian sub was nowhere in sight; probably it had landed the men and backed out of danger from any unexpected quarter. Two or three corpses lay in view, down by the water's edge. From where I stood I couldn't say if they were good guys or bad. There were more shots, coming from somewhere off to the left. It looked like the boys were fighting it out old style: hand to hand, with small arms. It figured; after all, what they wanted was me and all my clever ideas, intact, not a smoking ruin.

I don't know whether it was my romantic streak or my cynical one that had made me drive the architect nuts putting secret passages in the walls of my chateau and tunnels under the lawn, but I was very glad now I had them. There was a narrow door in the west wall of the strong-room that gave onto a tight spiral stair. From there, I could take my choice: the boathouse, the edge of the woods behind the house, or the beach a hundred yards north of the jetty. All I had to do was—

THE house trembled a split second ahead of a terrific blast that slammed me to the floor. I felt blood start from my nose. Head ringing, I scrambled to my feet, groped through the dust to my escape hatch. Somebody outside was getting impatient.

My fingers were on the sensitive pressure areas that worked the concealed door. I took a last glance around the room, where the dust was just settling from the last blast. My eyes fell on the cylinder, lying where I had tossed it. In one jump I was across the room and had grabbed it up. I had found it aboard the lifeboat, concealed among the bones of the man with the bear-tooth necklace. Now I, with my Vallonian memories banked in my mind, could appreciate just how precious an object it was. It was Foster's memory. It would be only a copy, undoubtedly; still, I couldn't leave it behind.

A blast heavier than the last one rocked the house. Snorting and coughing from the dust, I got back to the emergency door, went through it, and started down.

The fight was going on, as near as I could judge, to the south of the house and behind it. Probably the woods were full of skirmishers, taking advantage of the cover. The best bet was the boathouse, direct. With a little luck I'd find my boat intact.

THE tunnel was dark but that didn't bother me. It ran dead straight to the boathouse. I came to the wooden slat door and stood for a moment, listening; everything was quiet. I eased it open and stepped onto the ramp, inside the building. In the gloom, polished mahogany and chromework threw back muted highlights. I circled, slipped the mooring rope, and was about to step into the cockpit when I heard the bolt of a rifle snick home. I whirled, threw myself flat. The deafening bam of a .30 calibre fired at close quarters laid a pattern of fine ripples on the black water. I rolled, hit with a splash that drowned a second shot, and dove deep. Three strokes took me under the door, out into the green gloom of open water. I hugged the yellowish sand of the bottom, angled off to the right, and kept going.

I had to get out of my jacket, and somehow I managed it, almost without losing a stroke. And there went all the goodies I'd stashed away in the pockets, down to the bottom of the drink. I still had the memory-trace in my slacks. I managed thirty strokes before having to surface. I got half a gulp of fresh air before the shot slapped spray into my face and echoed off across the water. I sank like a stone, kicked off, and made another twenty-five yards before I had to come up. The rifleman was faster this time. The bullet creased my shoulder like a hot iron, and I was under water again. My kickwork was weak now; the strength was draining from my arms fast. I had to have air. My chest was on fire and there was a whirling blackness all around me. I felt consciousness fading...

*As from a distance I observed the clumsy efforts of the swimmer, watched the flounderings of the poor, untrained creature...*

*It was apparent that an override of the autonomic system was required. With dispatch I activated cortical area omicron, rerouted the blood supply, drew an emergency oxygen source from stored fats, diverting the necessary energy to break the molecular bonds.*

*Now, with the body drawing on internal sources, ample for six hundred seconds; at maximum demand, I stimulated areas upsilon and mu. I channeled full survival-level energy to the muscle complexes involved, increased power output to full skeletal tolerance, eliminated waste motion.*

*The body drove through the water with the fluid grace of a sea-denizen...*

I FLOATED on my back, breathing in great surges of cool air and blinking at the crimson sky. I had been under water, a few yards from shore, drowning. Then there was an awareness, like a voice, telling me what to do. From out of the mass of Valllonian knowledge I had acquired, I had drawn what I needed. And now I was here, half a mile from the beach, winded but intact. I felt beat and hungry, but I had to keep my mind on the problem of getting to the mainland. It was a fifteen-mile swim, but if the boys on shore could keep each other occupied, I ought to be able to make it. The full moon would make steering easy. And the first thing I would do when I got out of this would be to order the biggest, rarest steak in South America.

## CHAPTER ELEVEN

I SAT at the kitchen table in Margareta's Lima apartment and gnawed the last few shreds off the stripped T-bone, while she poured me another cup of coffee.

"Now tell me about it," she said. "You say they burned your house, but why? And how did you get here?"

"They got so interested in the fight, they lost their heads," I said. "That's the only explanation I can think of. I figured they'd go to some pains to avoid damaging me. I guessed wrong."

"But your own people..."

"Maybe they were right: they couldn't afford to let the Russkis get me."

"But how did you get covered with mud? And the blood stains on your back?"

"I had a nice long swim: five hours worth. Then another hour getting through a mangrove swamp. Lucky I had a moon. Then a three-hour hike..."

"You'd better get some sleep," said Margareta. "What do you want me to do?"

"Get me some clothes," I said. "A grey suit, white shirt, black tie and shoes. And go to my bank and draw some money, say five thousand. Oh yeah, see if there's anything in the papers. If you see anybody hanging around the lobby when you comeback, don't come up; give me a call and I'll meet you."

She stood up. "This is really awful," she said. "Can't your embassy—"

"Didn't I mention it? A Mr. Pruffy, of the embassy, came along to hold Smale's hand...not to mention a Colonel Sanchez. I wouldn't be surprised if the local cops weren't in the act by now..."

"Where will you go?"

"I'll get to the airport and play it by ear. I don't think they've alerted everybody. It was a hush-hush deal, until it went sour; now they're still picking up the pieces."

"The bank won't be open for hours yet," said Margareta. "Go to sleep and don't worry. I'll take care of everything."

I KNEW I wasn't alone as soon as I opened my eyes. I hadn't heard anything, but I could feel someone in the room. I sat up slowly, looked around.

He was sitting in the embroidered chair by the window: an ordinary-looking fellow in a tan tropical suit, with an unlighted cigarette in his mouth and no particular expression on his face.

"Go ahead, light up," I said. "Don't mind me."

"Thanks," he said, in a thin voice. He took a lighter from an inner pocket, flipped it, held it to the cigarette.

I stood up. There was a blur of motion from my visitor, and the lighter was gone and a short-nosed revolver was in its place.

"You've got the wrong scoop, mister," I said. "I don't bite."

"I'd rather you wouldn't move suddenly, Mr. Legion."

"Which side are you working for?" I asked. "And can I put my shoes on.

He rested the pistol on his knee. "Get completely dressed, Mr. Legion."

"Sorry," I said. "No can do. No clothes."

He frowned slightly. "My jacket will be a little small for you," he said. "But I think you can manage."

"How come you didn't figure I was dead?" I asked.

"We checked the house," he said. "No body."

"Why, you incompetent asses. You were supposed to think I drowned."

"That possibility was considered. But we made the routine checks anyway."

"Nice of you to let me sleep it out. How long have you been here?"

"Only a few minutes," he said. He glanced at his watch. "We'll have to be going in another fifteen."

"What do you want with me?" I said. "You blew up everything you were interested in."

"The Department wants to ask you a few questions."

I looked at the pistol. "I wonder if you'd really shoot me," I mused.

"I'll try to make the position clear," he said, "just to avoid any unfortunate misunderstanding. My instructions are to bring you in, alive—if possible. If it appears that you may evade arrest...or fall into the wrong hands, I'll be forced to use the gun."

I PULLED my shoes on, thinking it over. My best chance to make a break was now, while there was only one watch dog. But I had a feeling he was telling the truth about shooting me. I had already seen the boys in action at the house.

He got up. "Let's step into the living room, Mr. Legion," he said. I moved past him through the door. In the living room the clock on the mantle said eleven. I'd been asleep for five or six hours. Margareta ought to be getting back any minute...

"Put this on," he said. I took the light jacket and wedged myself into it.

The telephone rang.

I looked at my watchdog. He shook his head. We stood and listened to it ring. After a while it stopped.

"We'd better be going now," he said. "Walk ahead of me, please. We'll take the elevator to the basement and leave by the service entrance—"

He stopped talking, eyes on the door. There was the rattle of a key. The gun came up.

"Hold it," I snapped. "It's the girl who owns the apartment." I moved to face him, my back to the door.

"That was foolish of you, Legion," he said. "Don't move again."

I watched the door in the big mirror on the opposite wall. The knob turned, the door swung in...and a thin brown man in white shirt and white pants slipped into the room. As he pushed the door back he transferred a small automatic to his left hand. My keeper threw a lever on the revolver that was aimed at my belt buckle.

"Stand absolutely still, Legion," he said. "If you have a chance, that's it." He moved aside slightly, looked past me to the newcomer. I watched in the mirror as the man in white behind me swiveled to keep both of us covered.

"This is a fail-safe weapon," said my first owner to the new man. "I think you know about them. We leaked the information to you. I'm holding the trigger back; if my hand relaxes, it fires; so I'd be a little careful about shooting, if I were you."

The thin man swallowed. He didn't say anything. He was having to make some tough decisions. His instructions would be the same as my other friend's: to bring me in alive, if possible.

"Who does this bird represent?" I asked my man.

"He's a Soviet agent."

I looked in the mirror at the man again. "Nuts," I said. "He looks like a waiter in a chile joint. He probably came up to take our order."

"You talk too much," said my keeper between his teeth. He held the gun on me steadily. I watched his trigger finger to see if it looked like relaxing.

"I'd say it's a stalemate," I said. "Let's take it once more from the top. Both of you go—"

"Shut up, Legion." My man licked his lips, glanced at my face. "I'm sorry. It looks as though—"

"You don't want to shoot me," I blurted out, loudly. In the mirror I had seen the door, which was standing ajar, ease open an inch, two inches. "You'll spoil this nice coat..." I kept on talking: "And anyway it would be a big mistake, because everybody knows Russian agents are stubby men with wide cheekbones and tight hats—"

SILENTLY, Margareta slipped into the room, took two quick steps, and slammed, a heavy handbag down on the slicked-back pompadour that went with the Adam's apple. Then man in white stumbled and fired a round into the rug.

The automatic dropped from his hand, and my pal in tan stepped to him and hit him hard on the back of the head with his pistol. He whirled toward me, hissed, "Play it smart" just loud enough for me to hear, then turned to Margareta. He slipped the gun in his pocket, but I knew he could get it out again in a hurry.

"Very nicely done, Miss," he said. "I'll have this person removed from your apartment. Mr. Legion and I were just going."

Margareta looked at me. I didn't want to see her get hurt —or involved.

"It's okay, honey," I said. "This is Mr. Jones...of our Embassy. We're old friends." I stepped past her, headed for the door. My hand was on the knob when I heard a solid thunk behind me. I whirled in time to clip the FBI on the jaw as he fell forward. Margareta looked at me, wide-eyed.

"That handbag packs a wallop," I said. "Nice work, Maggie." I knelt, pulled off the fellow's belt, and cinched his hands behind his back with it. Margareta got the idea, did the same for the other man, who was beginning to groan now.

"Who are these men?" she asked.

"I'll tell you all about it later. Right now, I have to get to some people I know, get this story on the wires, out in the open. State'll be a little shy about gunning me down or locking me up without trial, if I give the show enough publicity." I reached in my pocket, handed her the black-&-gold-marked cylinder. Mail this to—Joe Dugan—at Itzenca, general delivery."

"All right," Margareta said. "And I have your things." She stepped into the hall, came back with a shopping bag and a suit carton. She took a wad of bills from her handbag and handed it to me.

I went to her and put my arms around her. "Listen,

honey: as soon as I leave go to the bank and draw fifty grand. Get out of the country. They haven't got anything on you except that you beaned a couple of intruders in your apartment, but it'll be better if you disappear. Leave an address care of Poste Restante, Basle, Switzerland. I'll get in touch when I can."

Twenty minutes later I was pushing through the big glass doors onto the sidewalk, clean shaven, dressed to the teeth, with five grand on one hip and a .32 on the other. I'd had a good meal and a fair sleep, and against me the secret services of two or three countries didn't have a chance.

I got as far as the corner before they nailed me.

## CHAPTER TWELVE

"YOU have a great deal to lose," General Smale was saying, "and nothing to gain by your stubbornness. You're a young man, vigorous and, I'm sure, intelligent. You have a fortune of some million and a quarter dollars, which I assure you you'll be permitted to keep. As against that prospect, so long as you refuse to co-operate, we must regard you as no better than a traitorous criminal—and deal with you accordingly."

"What have you been feeding me?" I said. "My mouth tastes like somebody's old gym shoes and my arm's purple to the elbow. Don't you know it's illegal to administer drugs without a license?"

"The nation's security is at stake," snapped Smale.

"The funny thing is, it must not have worked, or you wouldn't be begging me to tell all. I thought that scopolamine or whatever you're using was the real goods."

"We've gotten nothing but gibberish," Smale said, "most of it in an incomprehensible language. Who the devil are you, Legion? Where do you come from?"

"You know everything," I said. "You told me so yourself. I'm a guy named Legion, from Mount Sterling, Illinois, population: one thousand eight hundred and ninety-two."

Smale had gone white. "I'm in a position to inflict agonies on you, you insolent rotter," he grated. "I've refrained from doing so. I'm a soldier; I know my duty. I'm prepared to give my life; if need be, my honor, to obtain for my government the information you're withholding."

"Turn me loose; then ask me in a nice way. As far as I know, I haven't got anything of military significance to tell you, but if I were treated as a free citizen I might be inclined to let you be the judge of that."

"Tell us now; then you'll go free."

"Sure," I said. "I invented a combination rocket ship and time machine. I traveled around the solar system and made a few short trips back into history. In my spare time I invented other gadgets. I'm planning to take out patents, so naturally I don't intend to spill any secrets. Can I go now?"

Smale got to his feet. "Until we can safely move you, you'll remain in this room. You're on the sixty-third floor of the Yordano Building. The windows are of unbreakable glass, in case you contemplate a particularly untidy suicide. Your person has been stripped of all potentially dangerous items. The door is of heavy construction and securely locked. The furniture has been removed so you can't dismantle it for use as a weapon. It's rather a drab room to spend your future in, but until you decide to cooperate this will be your world."

I DIDN'T say anything. I sat on the floor and watched him leave. I caught a glimpse of two uniformed men outside the door. No doubt they'd take turns looking through the peephole. I'd have solitude without privacy.

I stretched out on the floor, which was padded with a nice thick rug, presumably so that I wouldn't beat my brains out against it just to spite them. I was way behind on my sleep: being interrogated while unconscious wasn't a very restful procedure. I wasn't too worried. In spite of what Smale said, they couldn't keep me here forever. Maybe Margareta had gotten clear and told the story to some newsmen; this kind of thing couldn't stay hidden forever. Or could it?

I thought about what Smale had said about my talking gibberish under the narcotics. That was an odd one...

Quite suddenly I got it. By means of the drugs they must have tapped a level where the Vallonian background briefing was stored: they'd been firing questions at a set of memories that didn't speak English. I grinned, then laughed out loud. Luck was still in the saddle with me.

The glass was in double panels, set in aluminum frames and sealed with a plastic strip. The space between the two panels of glass was evacuated of air, creating an insulating barrier against the heat of the sun. I ran a finger over the aluminum. It was dural: good tough stuff. If I had something to pry with, I might possibly lever the metal away from the glass far enough to take a crack at the edge, the weak point of armor-glass...if I had something to hit it with.

Smale had done a good job of stripping the room—and me. I had my shirt and pants and shoes, but no tie or belt. I still had my wallet—empty, a pack of cigarettes with two wilted weeds in it, and a box of matches. Smale had missed a bet: I might set fire to my hair and burn to the ground. I might also stuff a sock, down my throat and strangle, or hang myself with a shoelace—but I wasn't going to.

I looked at the window some more. The door was too tough to tackle, and the heavies outside were probably hoping for an excuse to work me over. They wouldn't expect me to go after the glass; after all, I was still sixty-three stories up. What would I do if I did make it to the window sill? But we could worry about that later, after I had smelled the fresh air.

My forefinger found an irregularity in the smooth metal: a short groove. I looked closer, saw a screw head set flush with the aluminum surface. Maybe if the frame was bolted together—

No such luck; the screw I had found was the only one. What was it for? Maybe if I removed it I'd find out. But I'd wait until dark to try it. Smale hadn't left a light fixture in the room. After sundown I'd be able to work unobserved.

A COUPLE of hours went by and no one came to disturb my solitude, not even to feed me. I had a short scrap of metal I'd worked loose from my wallet. It was mild steel, flimsy stuff, only about an inch long, but I was hoping the screw might not be set too tight. Aluminum threads strip pretty easily, so it probably wasn't cinched up too hard.

There was no point in theorizing. It was dark now; I'd give it a try. I went to the window, fitted the edge of metal into the slotted screw-head, and twisted. It turned, just like that. I backed it off ten turns, twenty; it was a thick bolt with fine threads. It came free and air whooshed into the hole. The screw apparently sealed the panel after the air was evacuated.

I thought it over. If I could fill the space between the panels with water and let it freeze...quite a trick in the tropics. I might as well plan to fill it with gin and set it on fire.

I was going in circles. Every idea I got started with "if", I needed something I could manage with the materials at hand:

cloth, a box of matches, a few bits of paper.

I got out a cigarette, lit up, and while the match was burning examined the hole from which I'd removed the plug. It was about three sixteenths of an inch in diameter and an inch deep, and there was a hole near the bottom communicating with the air space between the glass panels. It was an old-fashioned method of manufacture but it seemed to have worked all right: the air was pumped out and the hole sealed with the screw. It had at any rate the advantage of being easy to service if the panel leaked. Now with some way of pumping air *in*, I could blowout the panels...

There was no pump on the premises but I did have some chemicals: the match heads. They were old style too, like a lot of things in Peru: the strike-once-and-throw-away kind.

I sat on the floor and started to work, chipping the heads off the matchsticks, collecting the dry, purplish material on a scrap of paper. Thirty-eight matches gave me a respectable sample. I packed it together, rolled it in the paper, and crimped the ends. Then I tucked the makeshift firecracker into the hole the screw had come from.

Using the metal scrap I scraped at the threads of the screw, blurring them. Then I started it in the hole, half a dozen turns, until it came up against the match heads.

The shoes Margareta had bought me had built-up leather heels: hell on the feet, but just the thing to pound with.

I TOOK the shoe by the toe and hefted it: the flexible sole gave it a good action, like a well-made sap. There were still a couple of "if's" in the equation, but a healthy crack on the screw ought to drive it against the packed match-heads hard enough to detonate them, and the expanding gasses from the explosion ought to exert enough pressure against the glass panels to break them. I'd know in a second.

I flattened myself against the wall, brought the shoe up,

and laid it on the screw-head.

There was a deafening boom, a blast of hot air, and a chemical stink, then a gust of cool night wind—and I was on the sill, my back to the street six hundred feet below, my fingers groping for a hold on the ledge above the window. I found a grip, pulled up, reached higher, got my feet on the muntin strip, paused to rest for three seconds, reached again...

I pulled my feet above the window level and heard shouts in the room below:

"—fool killed himself!"

"Get a light in here!"

I clung, breathing deep, and murmured thanks to the architect who had stressed a strong horizontal element in his facade and arranged the strip windows in bays set twelve inches from the face of the structure. Now, if the boys below would keep their eyes on the street underneath long enough for me to get to the roof—

I looked up, to get an idea how far I'd have to go—and gripped the ledge convulsively as the whole building leaned out, tilting me back...

Cold sweat ran into my eyes. I squeezed the stone until my knuckles creaked, and held on. I laid my cheek against the rough plaster, listened to my heart thump. Adrenalin and high hopes had gotten me this far...and now it had all drained out and left me, a frail ground-loving animal, flattened against the cruel face of a tower like a fly on a ceiling, with nothing between me and the unyielding concrete below but the feeble grip of fingers and toes. I started to yell for help, and the words stuck in my dry throat. I breathed in shallow gasps, feeling my muscles tightening, until I hung, rigid as a board, afraid even to roll my eyeballs for fear of dislodging myself. I closed my eyes, felt my hands going numb, and tried again to yell: only a thin croak.

A minute earlier I had had only one worry: that they'd look up and see me. Now my worst fear was that they wouldn't.

This was the end. I'd been close before, but not like this. My fingers could take the strain for maybe another minute, maybe even two; then I'd let go, and the wind would whip at me for a few timeless seconds, before I hit.

DOWN inside of me a small defiance flickered, found a foothold, burned brighter. I would die...but Hell that would solve a lot of problems. And if I had to die, at least I could die trying.

My mind moved in to take over from my body. It was the body that was wasting my last strength on a precarious illusion of safety, numbing my senses, paralyzing me. It was a tyranny I wouldn't accept. I needed a cool head and a steady hand and an unimpaired sense of balance; and if the imbecile boy wouldn't cooperate the mind would damn well force it. First: loosen the grip—Yes! if it killed me: bend those fingers!

I was standing a little looser now, my hands resting flat, my legs taking the load. I had a good wide ledge to stand on: nearly a foot, and in a minute I was going to reach up and get a new hold, and lift one foot at a time...and if I slipped, at least I'd have done it my way.

I let go, and the building leaned out, and to hell with it.

. . .

I felt for the next ledge, gripped it, pulled up, found a toehold.

Sure, I was dead. It was a long way to the top, and there was a fancy cornice I'd never get over, but when the moment came and I started the long ride down I'd thumb my nose at the old hag, Instinct, who hadn't been as tough as she thought she was.

...

I WAS under the cornice now, hanging on for a breather and listening to the hooting and hollering from the window far below. A couple of heads had popped out and taken a look, but it was dark up where I was and all the attention was centered down where the crowd had gathered and lights were playing, looking for the mess. Pretty soon now they'd begin to get the drift—so I'd better be going.

I looked up at the overhang...and felt the old urge to clutch and hang on. So I leaned outward a little further, just to show me who was boss. It was a long reach, and I'd have to risk it all on one lunge because, if I missed, there wasn't any net, and my fingers knew it; I heard my nails rasp on the plaster. I grated my teeth together and unhooked one hand: it was like a claw carved from wood. I took a half-breath, bent my knees slightly; they were as responsive as a couple of bumper-jacks bolted on at the hip. Tough; but it was now or never...

I let go with both hands and stretched, leaning back...

My wooden hands bumped the edge, scrabbled, hooked on, as my legs swung free, and I was hanging like an old-time sailor strung up by the thumbs. A wind off the roof whipped at my face and now I was a tissue-paper doll, fluttering in the breeze.

I HAD to pull now, pull hard, heave myself up and over the edge, but I was tired, too tired, and a dark curtain was falling over me...

Then from the darkness a voice was speaking in a strange language: a confusion of strange thought symbols, but through them an ever more insistent call:

...*dilate the secondary vascular complex, shunt full conductivity to the upsilon neurochannel. Now, stripping oxygen ions from fatty cell masses, pour in electro-chemical energy to the sinews...*

With a smooth surge of power I pulled myself up, fell forward, rolled onto my back, and lay on the flat roof, the beautiful flat roof, still warm from the day's sun.

I was here, looking at the stars, safe, and later on when I had more time I'd stop to think about it. But now I had to move, before they'd had time to organize themselves, cordon off the building, and start a door-to-floor search.

Staggering a bit from the exertion of the long climb I got to my feet, went to the shed housing the entry to the service stair. A short flight of steps led down to a storeroom. There were dusty boards, dried-up paint cans; odd tools. I picked up a five-foot length of two-by-four and a hammer with one claw missing, and stepped out into the hall. The street was a long way down and I didn't feel like wasting time with stairs. I found the elevator, got in and pushed the button for the foyer.

IN a few seconds it stopped and the doors opened. I glanced out, tightened my grip on the hammer, and stepped out. I could see the lights in the street out front and in the distance there was the wail of a siren, but nobody in the lobby looked my way. I headed across toward the side exit, dumped the board at the door, tucked the hammer in the waistband of my pants, and stepped out onto the pavement. There were a lot of people hurrying past but this was Lima: they didn't waste a glance on a bare-footed carpenter.

I moved off, not hurrying. There was a lot of rough country between me and Itzenca, the little town near which the lifeboat was hidden in a canyon, but I aimed to cover it in a week. Some time between now and tomorrow I'd have to figure out a way to equip myself with a few necessities, but I wasn't worried. A man who had successfully taken up human-fly work in middle life wouldn't have any trouble stealing a pair of boots.

Foster had shoved off for home three years ago, local time, although to him, aboard the ship, only a few weeks might have passed. My lifeboat was a midge compared to the mother ship he rode, but it had plenty of speed. Once aboard the lugger...and maybe I could put a little space between me and the big boys.

I had used the best camouflage I knew of on the boat. The near-savage native bearers who had done my unloading and carried my Vallonian treasures across the desert to the nearest railhead were not the gossipy type. If General Smale's boys had heard about the boat, they hadn't mentioned it. And if they had: well, I'd solve that one when I got to it. There were still quite a few 'if's' in the equation, but my arithmetic was getting better all the time.

## CHAPTER THIRTEEN

I TOOK the precaution of sneaking up on the lifeboat in the dead of night, but I could have saved myself a crawl. Except for the fact that the camouflage nets had rotted away to shreds, the ship was just as I had left it, doors sealed. Why Smale's team hadn't found it, I didn't know; I'd think that one over when I was well away from Earth.

I went into the post office at Itzenca to pick up the parcel Margareta had mailed me with Foster's memory-trace in it. While I was checking to see whether Uncle Sam's minions had intercepted the package and substituted a carrot, I felt something rubbing against my shin. I glanced down and saw a grey and white cat, reasonably clean and obviously hungry. I don't know whether I'd ploughed through a field of wild catnip the night before or if it was my way with a finger behind the furry ears, but kitty followed me out of Itzenca and right into the bush. She kept pace with me, leading most of the time, as far as the space boat, and was the first one aboard.

I didn't waste time with formalities. I had once audited a briefing rod on the boat's operation—not that I had ever expected to use the information for a take-off. Once aboard, I hit the controls and cut a swathe through the atmosphere that must have sent fingers jumping for panic buttons from Washington to Moscow.

I didn't know how many weeks or months of unsullied leisure stretched ahead of me now. There would be time to spare for exploring the boat, working out a daily routine, chewing over the details of both my memories, and laying plans for my arrival on Foster's world, Vallon. But first I wanted to catch a show that was making a one-night stand for me only: the awe-inspiring spectacle of the retreating Earth.

I DROPPED into a seat opposite the screen and flipped into view the big luminous ball of wool that was my home planet. I'd been hoping to get a last look at my island, but I couldn't see it. The whole sphere was blanketed in cloud: a thin worn blanket in places but still intact. But the moon was a sight! An undipped Edam cheese with the markings of Roquefort. For a quarter of an hour I watched it grow until it filled my screen. It was too close for comfort. I dumped the tabby out of my lap and adjusted a dial. The dead world swept past, and I had a brief glimpse of blue burst bubbles of craters that became the eyes and mouth and pock marks of a face on a head that swung away from me in disdain and then the sibling planets dwindled and were gone forever.

The lifeboat was completely equipped, and I found comfortable quarters. An ample food supply was available by the touch of a panel on the table in the screen room. That was a trick my predecessor with the dental jewelry hadn't discovered, I guessed. During the course of my first journey earthward and on my visits to the boat for saleable playthings while she lay in dry-dock, I had discovered most of the available amenities aboard. Now I luxuriated in a steaming bath of recycled water, sponged down with disposable towels packed in scented alcohol, fed the cat and myself, and lay down to sleep for about two weeks.

By the third week I was reasonably refreshed and rested. The cat was a godsend, I began to realize. I named her Itzenca, after the village where she adopted me, and I talked to her by the hour.

"Say, Itz," said I, "where would you like your sand box situated? Right there in front of the TV screen?"

No, said Itzenca by a flirt of her tail. And she walked over behind a crate that had never been unloaded on earth.

I pulled out a box of junk and slid the sand-box in its place. Itzenca promptly lost interest and instead jumped up on the junk box, which fell off the bench and scattered small objects of khaff and metal in all directions.

"Come back here, blast you," I said, "and help me pick up this stuff."

Itz bounded after a dull-gleaming silver object that was still rolling. I was there almost as quick as she was and grabbed up the cylinder. Suddenly horsing around was over. This thing was somebody's memory.

I DROPPED onto a bench to examine it, my Vallonian-inspired pulse pounding. Itz jumped up into my lap and nosed the cylinder. I was trying to hark back to those days three years before when I had loaded the lifeboat with all the loot it would carry, for the trip back to Earth.

"Listen, Itz, we've got to do some tall remembering. Let's see: there was a whole rack of blanks in the memory-recharging section of the room where we found the three skeletons. Yeah, now I remember: I pulled this one out of the recorder set. I showed it to Foster when he was hunting his own trace. He didn't realize I'd pulled it out of the machine and he thought it was an empty. But I'll bet you somebody had his mind taped, and then left in a hurry, before the trace could be color-coded and filed.

"On the other hand, maybe it's a blank that had just been inserted when somebody broke up the play-house... But wasn't there something Foster said...about when he woke up, way back when, with a pile of fresh corpses around him? He gave somebody emergency treatment and to a Vallonian that would include a complete memory-transcription... Do you realize what I've got here in my hand, Itz?"

She looked up at me inquiringly.

"This is what's left of the guy that Foster buried: his pal, Ammaerln, I think he called him. What's inside his cylinder used to be tucked away in the skull of the Ancient Sinner. The guy's not so dead after all. I'll bet his family will pay plenty for this trace, and be grateful besides. That'll be an ace in the hole in case I get too hungry on Vallon."

I got up, crossed the apartment and dropped the trace in a drawer beside Foster's own memory.

"Wonder how Foster's making out without his past, Itz? He claimed the one I've got here could only be a copy of the original stored at Okk-Hamiloth, but my briefing didn't say anything about copying memories. He must be somebody pretty important to rate that service."

Suddenly my eyes were riveted to the markings on Foster's

trace lying in the drawer. "Zblood! The royal colors!" I sat down on the bed with a lurch. "Itzenca, old gal, it looks like we'll be entering Vallonian society from the top. We've been consorting with a member of the Vallonian nobility!"

DURING the days that followed, I tried again and again to raise Foster on the communicator...without result. I wondered how I'd find him among the millions on the planet. My best bet would be to get settled down in the Vallonian environment, then start making a few inquiries.

I would play it casually: act the part of a Vallonian who had merely been travelling for a few hundred years—which wasn't unheard of—and play my cards close to my gravy stains until I learned what the score was. With my Vallonian briefing I ought to be able to carry it off. The Vallonians might not like illegal immigrants any better than they did back home, so I'd keep my interesting foreign background to myself.

I would need a new name. I thought over several possibilities and selected "Drgon." It was certainly as good a Vallonian jawbreaker as any.

I canvassed the emergency wardrobe that was standard equipment on Far-Voyager lifeboats and picked one in a sober color, then got busy with the cutting and seaming unit to fit it to my frame.

* * *

The proximity alarms were ringing. I watched the screen with its image of a great green world rimmed on one edge with glading white from the distant giant sun, on the other, flooded with a cool glow reflected from the blue outer planet.

The trip was almost over and my confidence was beginning to fray around the edges. In a few minutes I would be stepping into an unknown world, all set to find my old pal Foster and see the sights. I didn't have a passport, but there was no reason to anticipate trouble. All I had to do was let my natural identity take a back seat and allow my Vallonian background to do the talking. And yet...

Now Vallon spread out below us, a misty grey-green landscape, bright under the glow of the immense moon-like sister world. I had set the landing monitor for Okk-Hamiloth, the capital city of Vallon. That was where Foster would have headed, I guessed. Maybe I could pick up the trail there.

The city was directly below: a vast network of blue-lit avenues. I hadn't been contacted by planetary control. That was normal, however. A small vessel coming in on auto could handle itself.

A little apprehensively I ran over my lines a last time: I was Drgon, citizen of the Two Worlds, back from a longer-than-average season of far-voyaging and in need of briefing rods to bring me up to date on developments at home. I also required assignment of quarters...and directions to the nearest beerjoint. My tailoring was impeccable, my command of the language a little rusty from long non-use, and the only souvenirs I had to declare were a tattered native costume from my last port of call, a quaint weapon from the same, and a small animal I had taken a liking to.

THE landing-ring was visible on the screen now, coming slowly up to meet us. There was a gentle shock and then absolute stillness. I watched the port cycle open; I went to it and looked out at the pale city stretching away to the hills. I took a breath of the fragrant night air that was spiced with a long-forgotten perfume, and the part of me that was now

Vallonian ached with the inexpressible emotion of homecoming.

I started to buckle on my pistol and gather up a few belongings, then decided to wait until I'd met the welcoming committee. I whistled to Itzenca and we stepped out and down. We crossed the clipped green, luminous in the glow from the lights over the high-arched gate marking the path that curved up toward the bright-lit terraces above. There was no one in sight. Bright Cintelight showed me the gardens and walks and, when I reached the terraces, the avenues beyond...but no people.

The cat and I walked across the terrace, passed through the open arch to a refreshment lounge. The low tables and cushioned couches stood empty under the rosy light from the ceiling panels.

I stood and listened: dead silence. The lights glowed, the tables waited invitingly. How long had they waited?

I sat down at one of them and thought hard. I had made a lot of plans, but I hadn't counted on a deserted spaceport. How was I going to ask questions about Foster if there was no one to ask?

I got up and moved on through the empty lounge, past a wide arcade, out onto a terraced lawn. A row of tall poplar-like trees made a dark wall beyond a still pool, and behind them distant towers loomed, colored lights sparkled. A broad avenue swept in a wide curve between fountains, slanted away to the hills. A hundred yards from where I stood a small vehicle was parked at the curb; I headed for it.

It was an open two-seater, low-slung, cushioned, finished in violet inlays against bright chrome. I slid into the seat, looked over the controls, while Itzenca skipped to a place beside me. There was a simple lever arrangement: a steering tiller. It looked easy. I tried a few pulls and pushes; lights blinked on the panel, the car quivered, lifted a few inches, drifted slowly across the road. I moved the tiller, twiddled things; the car moved off toward the towers.

TWO hours later we had cruised the city...and found nothing. It hadn't changed from what my extra memory recalled—except that all the people were gone. The parks and boulevards were trimmed, the fountains and pools sparkled, the lights glowed...but nothing moved. The automatic dust precipitators and air filters would run forever, keeping things clean and neat; but there was no one there to appreciate it. I pulled over, sat watching the play of colored lights on a waterfall, and considered. Maybe I'd find more of a clue inside one of the buildings. I left the car and picked one at random: a tall slab of pink crystal. Inside, I looked around at a great airy cavern full of rose-colored light and listened to the purring of the cat and my own breathing. There was nothing else to hear.

I picked a random corridor, went along it, passing through one empty room after another. I went out on a lofty terrace overlooking gardens, leaned on a balustrade, and looked up at the brilliant disc of Cinte.

"We've come a long way to find nothing," I said to Itzenca. She pushed her way along my leg and flexed her tail in a gesture meant to console.

I sat on the balustrade and leaned back against the polished pink wall, took out a clarinet I'd found in one of the rooms and blew some blue notes. That which once had been was no more; remembering it, I played the *Pavane for a Dead-Princess.*

I finished and looked up at a sound. Four tall men in grey cloaks and a glitter of steel came toward me from the shadows.

I HAD dropped the clarinet and was on my feet. I tried

to back up but the balustrade stopped me. The four spread out. The man in the lead fingered a wicked-looking short club and spoke to me—in gibberish. I blinked at him and tried to think of a snappy comeback.

He snapped his fingers and two of the others came up; they reached for my arms. I started to square off, fist cocked, then relaxed; after all, I was just a tourist, Drgon by name. Unfortunately, before I could get my fist back, the man with the club swung it and caught me across the forearm. I yelled, jumped back, found myself grappled by the others. My arm felt dead to the shoulder. I tried a kick and regretted that too; there was armor under the cloaks. The club wielder said something and pointed at the cat...

It was time I wised up. I relaxed, tried to coax my alter ego into the foreground. I listened to the rhythm of the language: it was Vallonian, badly warped by time, but I could understand it:

"—musician would be an Owner!" one of them said.

Laughter.

"Whose man are you, piper? What are your colors?"

I curled my tongue, tried to shape it around the sort of syllables I heard them uttering, but it seemed to me a gross debasement of the Vallonian I knew. Still I managed an answer:

"I...am a...citizen...of Vallon."

"A dog of a masterless renegade?" The man with the club hefted it, glowered at me. "And what wretched dialect is that you speak?"

"I have...been long a-voyaging," I stuttered. "I ask...for briefing rods...and for a...dwelling place."

"A dwelling place you'll have," the man said. "In the men's shed at Rath-Gallion." He gestured, and snapped handcuffs on me.

He turned and stalked away, and the others hustled me

after him. Over my shoulder I got a glimpse of a cat's tail disappearing over the balustrade. Outside, a long grey air car waited on the lawn. They dumped me in the back seat, climbed aboard. I got a last look at the spires of Okk-Hamiloth as we tilted, hurtled away across the low hills.

I had had an idealistic notion of wanting to fit into this new world, find a place in its society. I'd found a place all right: a job with security.

I was a slave.

# CHAPTER FOURTEEN

IT was banquet night at Rath-Gallion, and I gulped my soup in the kitchen and ran over in my mind the latest batch of jingles I was expected to perform. I had only been on the Estate a few weeks, but I was already Owner Gope's favorite piper. If I kept on at this rate, I would soon have a cell to myself in the slave pens.

Sime, the pastry cook, came over to me.

"Pipe us a merry tune, Drgon," he said, "and I'll reward you with a frosting pot."

"With pleasure, good Sime," I said. I finished off the soup and got out my clarinet. I had tried out half a dozen strange instruments, but I still liked this one best. "What's your pleasure?"

"One of the outland tunes you learned far-voyaging," called Cagu, the bodyguard.

I complied with the *Beer Barrel Polka*. They pounded the

table and hallooed when I finished, and I got my goody pan. Sime stood watching me scrape at it.

"Why don't you claim the Chief Piper's place, Drgon?" he said. "You pipe rings around the lout. Then you'd have freeman status, and could sit among us in the kitchen almost as an equal."

"I'd gladly be the equal of such a pastry cook as yourself," I said. "But what can a slave-piper do?"

Sime blinked at me. "You can challenge the Chief Piper," he said. "There's none can deny you're his master in all but name. Don't fear the outcome of the Trial; you'll triumph sure."

"But how can I claim another's place?" I asked.

Sime waved his arms. "You have far-voyaged long indeed, Piper Drgon. Know you naught of how the world wags these days? One would take you for a Cintean heretic."

"As I've said, in my youth all men were free; and the High King ruled at Okk-Hamiloth—"

"'Tis ill to speak of these things," said Sime in a low tone. "Only Owners know their former lives…though I've heard it said that long ago no man was so mean but that he recorded his lives and kept them safe. How you came by yours, I ask not; but do not speak of it. Owner Gope is a jealous master. Though a most generous and worshipful lord," he added hastily, looking around.

"I won't speak of it then, good Sime," I said. "But I have been long away. Even the language has changed, so that I wrench my tongue in the speaking of it. Advise me, if you will."

Sime puffed out his cheeks, frowning at me. "I scarce know where to start," he said. "All things belong to the Owners…as is only right. Men of low skill are likewise property; and 'tis well 'tis so; else would they starve as masterless strays…if the Greymen failed to find them first."

He made a sign and spat.

"NOW men of good skill are freemen, each earning rewards as befits his ability. I am Chief Pastry Cook to the Lord Gope, with the perquisites of that station, therefore, that none other equals my talents."

"And if some varlet claims the place of any man here," put in Cagu, "then he gotta submit to the trial."

"Then," said Sime, "this upstart pastry cook must cook against me; and all in the Hall will judge; and he who prevails is the Chief Pastry Cook, and the other takes a dozen lashes for his impertinence."

"But fear not, Drgon," spoke Cagu. "A Chief Piper ain't but a five-stroke man. Only a tutor is lower down among freemen."

There was a bellow from the door, and I grabbed my clarinet and scrambled after the page. Owner Gope didn't like to wait around for piper-slaves. I saw him looming up at his place, as I darted through to my assigned position within the huge circle of the viand-loaded table. The Chief Piper had just squeezed his bagpipe-like instrument and released a windy blast of discordant sound. He was a lean, squint-eyed rascal fond of ordering the slave-pipers about. He pranced in an intricate pattern, pumping away at his vari-colored bladders, until I winced at the screech of it. Owner Gope noticed him about the same time. He picked up a heavy brass mug and half rose to peg it at the Chief Piper, who saw it just in time to duck. The mug hit a swollen air-bag; it burst with a sour bleat.

"As sweet a note as has been played tonight," roared Owner Gope. "Begone, lest you call up the hill devils—"

His eye fell on me. "Now here's a true piper. Summon up a fair melody, Drgon, to clear the fumes of the last performer from the air before the wine sours."

I bowed low, wet my lips, and launched into the *One O' Clock Jump*. To judge from the roar that went up when I finished, they liked it. I followed with *Little Brown Jug* and *String of Pearls*. Gope pounded and the table quieted down.

"The rarest slave in all Rath-Gallion, I swear it," he bellowed. "Were he not a slave, I'd drink to his health."

"By your leave, Owner?" I said.

Gope stared, then nodded indulgently. "Speak then."

"I claim the place of Chief Piper. I—"

Yells rang out; Gope grinned widely.

"So be it," he said. "Shall the vote be taken now, or must we submit to more of the vile bladderings ere we proclaim our good Drgon Chief Piper? Speak out."

"Proclaim him!" somebody shouted.

Gope slammed a huge hand against the table. "Bring Iylk, the Chief Piper, before me," he yelled.

The piper reappeared.

"The place of the Chief Piper is declared vacant," Gope said loudly. "—since the former Chief Piper has been advanced in degree to a new office. Let these air-bags be punctured," Gope cried. "I banish their rancid squeals forever from Rath-Gallion. Now, let all men know: this former piper is now Chief Fool to this household. Let him wear the broken bladders as a sign of his office." There was a roar of laughter, glad cries, whistles.

I gave them *Mairzy Doats* and the former piper capered gingerly. Owner Gope roared with laughter.

A great day for Rath-Gallion," Gope shouted. "By the horns of the sea-god, I have gained a prince of pipers and a king of fools! I proclaim them to be ten-lash men, and both shall have places at table henceforth!"

I LOOKED around the barbarically decorated hall, seeing things in a new way. There's nothing like a little slavery to make a man appreciate even a modest portion of freedom. Everything I had thought I knew about Vallon had been wrong: the centuries that passed had changed things—and not for the better. The old society that Foster knew was dead and buried. The old places and villas lay deserted, the spaceports unused. And the old system of memory-recording that Foster described was lost and forgotten. I didn't know what kind of a cataclysm could have plunged the seat of a galactic empire back into feudal darkness—but it had happened.

So far I hadn't found a trace of Foster. My questions had gotten me nothing but blank stares. Maybe Foster hadn't made it; there could have been an accident in space. Or perhaps he was somewhere on the opposite side of the world. Vallon was a big planet and communications were poor. Maybe Foster was dead. I could live out a long life here and never find the answers.

I remembered my own disappointment at the breakdown of my illusions that night at Okk-Hamiloth. How much more heartbreaking must have been Foster's experience when and if he had arrived back here.

And Foster's memory that I had been bringing him for a keepsake: what a laugh that was! Far from being a superfluous duplicate of a master trace to which he had expected easy access, my copy of the trace was now, with the vaults at Okk-Hamiloth sealed and forbidden, of the greatest possible importance to Foster—and there wasn't a machine left on the planet to play it on.

Well, I still meant to find Foster if it took me—

Owner Gope was humming loudly and tunelessly to himself. I knew the sign. I got ready to play again. Being Chief Piper probably wasn't going to be just a bowl of cherries, but at least I wasn't a slave now. I had a long way to go, but I was making progress.

OWNER Gope and I got along well. He took me everywhere he went. He was a shrewd old duck and he liked having such an unusual piper on hand. He had heard from the Greymen, the free-lance police force, how I had landed at the deserted port. He warned me, in an oblique way, not to let word get out that I knew anything about old times in Vallon. The whole subject was tabu—especially the old capital city and the royal palaces themselves. Small wonder that my trespassing there had brought the Greymen down on me in double quick time.

One afternoon several months after my promotion I dropped in at the kitchen. I was due to shove off with Owner Gope and his usual retinue for a visit to Bar-Ponderone, a big estate a hundred miles north of Rath-Gallion in the direction of Okk-Hamiloth. Sime and my other old cronies fixed me up with a healthy lunch and a bottle of melon wine, and warned me that it would be a rough trip; the stretch of road we'd be using was a favorite hangout of road pirates.

"What I don't understand," I said, "is why Gope doesn't mount a couple of guns on the car and blast his way through the raiders. Every time he goes off the Estate he's taking his life in his hands."

The boys were shocked. "Even piratical renegades would never dream of taking a man's life, good Drgon," Sime said. "Every Owner, far and near, would band together to hunt such miscreants down. And their own fellows would abet the hunters! Nay, none is so low as to steal all a man's lives."

"The corsairs themselves know full well that in their next life they may be simple goodmen—even slaves," the Chief Wine-Pourer put in. "For you know, good Drgon, that when a member of a pirate band suffers the Change the others lead the newman to an Estate, that he may find his place..."

"How often do these Changes come along?" I asked.

"It varies greatly. Some men, of great strength and moral power, have been known to go on unchanged for three or four hundred years. But the ordinary man lives a life of eighty to one hundred years." Sime paused. "Or it may be less. A life of travail and strife can end much sooner than one of peace and retirement. Or unusual vicissitudes can shorten a life remarkably. A cousin of mine, who was marooned on the Great Stony Place in the southern half-world and who wandered for three weeks without more to eat or drink than a small bag of wine, underwent the Change after only fourteen years. When he was found his face was lined and his hair had greyed, in the way that presages the Change. And it was not long before he fell in a fit, as one does, and slept for a night and a day. When he awoke he was a newman: young and knowing nothing."

"Didn't you tell him who he was?"

"Nay!" Sime lowered his voice. "You are much favored of Owner Gope, good Drgon, and rightly. Still, there are matters a man talks not of—"

"A newman takes a name and sets out to learn whatever trade he can," put in the Carver of Roasts. "By his own skills he can rise...as you have risen, good Drgon."

"Don't you have memory machines—or briefing rods?" I persisted. "Little black sticks: you touch them to your head and—"

Sime made a motion in the air. "I have heard of these wands: a forbidden relic of the Black Arts—"

"Nuts," I said. "You don't believe in magic, do you, Sime? The rods are nothing but a scientific development by your own people. How you've managed to lose all knowledge of your own past—"

Sime raised his hands in distress. "Good Drgon, press us not in these matters. Such things are forbidden."

I WENT on out to the car and climbed in to wait for Owner Gope. It was impossible to learn anything about Vallon's history from these goodmen. They knew nothing.

I had reached a few tentative conclusions on my own, however. My theory was that some sudden social cataclysm had broken down the system of personality reinforcement and memory recording that had given continuity to the culture. Vallonian society, based as it was on the techniques of memory preservation, had gradually disintegrated. Vallon was plunged into a feudal state resembling its ancient social pattern of fifty thousand years earlier, before development of memory recording.

The people, huddled together on Estates for protection from real or imagined perils and shunning the old villas and cities as tabu—except for those included in Estates—knew nothing of space travel and ancient history. Like Sime, they had no wish even to speak of such matters.

I might have better luck with my detective work on a big Estate like Bar-Ponderone. I was looking forward to today's trip.

Gope appeared, with Cagu and two other bodyguards, four dancing girls, and an extra-large gift hamper. They took their places and the driver started up and wheeled the heavy car out onto the highroad. I felt a pulse of excitement as we accelerated in the direction of Bar-Ponderone. Maybe at the end of the ride I'd hit paydirt.


WE were doing about fifty down a winding mountain road. As we rounded a curve, the wheels screeching from the driver's awkward, too-fast swing into the turn, we saw another car in the road a quarter of a mile ahead, not moving, but parked—sideways. The driver hit the brakes.

Behind us Owner Gope yelled, "Pirates! Don't slacken

your pace, driver. Ram the blackguards, if you must!"

The driver rolled his eyes, almost lost control, then gritted his teeth, reached out to switch off the anti-collision circuit and slam the speed control lever against the dash. I watched for two long heart beats as we roared straight for the blockading car, then I slid over and grabbed for the controls. The driver held on, frozen. I rared back and clipped him on the jaw. He crumpled into his corner, mouth open and eyes screwed shut, as I hit the auto-steer override and worked the tiller. It was an awkward position for steering, but I preferred it to hammering in at ninety per.

The car ahead was still sitting tight, now a hundred yards away, now fifty. I cut hard to the right, toward the rising cliff face; the car backed to block me. At the last instant I whipped to the left, barreled past with half an inch to spare, rocketed along the ragged edge with the left wheel rolling on air, then whipped back into the center of the road.

"Well done!" yelled Cagu.

"But they'll give chase!" Gope shouted. "Masterless swine!"

The driver had his eyes open now. "Crawl over me!" I barked. He mumbled and clambered past me and I slid into his seat, still clinging to the accelerator lever and putting up the speed. Another curve was coming up. I grabbed a quick look in the rear-viewer: the pirates were swinging around to follow us.

"Press on!" commanded Gope. "We're close to Bar-Ponderone; it's no more than five miles—"

"What kind of speed have they got?" I called back.

"They'll best us easy," said Cagu cheerfully.

"What's the road like ahead?"

"A fair road, straight and true, now that we've descended the mountain," answered Gope.

We squealed through the turn and hit a straightaway. A

curving road branched off ahead. "What's that?" I snapped.

"A winding trail," gasped the driver. "It comes on Bar-Ponderone, but by a longer way."

I gauged my speed, braked minutely, and cut hard. We howled up the steep slope, into a turn between hills.

Gope shouted. "What madness is this?!"

"We haven't got a chance on the straightaway," I called back. "Not in a straight speed contest." I whipped the tiller over, then back the other way, following the tight S-curves. I caught a glimpse of our pursuers, just heading into the side road behind us.

"Any way they can head us off?" I yelled.

"Not unless they have confederates stationed ahead," said Gope; "but these pariahs work alone."

I worked the brake and speed levers, handled the tiller. We swung right, then left, higher and higher, then down a steep grade and up again. The pirate car rounded a turn, only a few hundred yards behind now. I scanned the road ahead, followed its winding course along the mountainside, through a tunnel, then out again to swing around the shoulder of the next peak.

"Pitch something out when we go through the tunnel!" I yelled.

"My cloak," cried Gope. "And the gift hamper."

We roared into the tunnel mouth. There was a blast of air as the rear deck cover opened. Gope and Cagu hefted the heavy gift hamper, tumbled it out, followed it with a cloak, a wine jug, assorted sandals, bracelets, fruit. Then we were back in the sunlight and I was fighting the curve. In the rear-viewer I saw the pirates burst from the tunnel mouth, Gope's black and yellow cloak spread over the canopy, smashed fruit spattered over it, the remains of the hamper dragging under the chassis. The car rocked and a corner of the cloak lifted; clearing the driver's view barely in time.

"Tough luck," I said. "We've got a long straight stretch ahead, and I'm fresh out of ideas..."

THE other car gained. I held the speed bar against the dash but we were up against a faster car; it was a hundred yards behind us, then fifty, then pulling out to go alongside. I slowed imperceptibly, let him get his front wheels past us, then cut sharply. Here was a clash of wheel fairings, and I fought the tiller as we rebounded from the heavier car. He crept forward, almost alongside again; shoulder to shoulder we raced at ninety-five down the steep grade..."

I hit the brakes and cut hard to the left, slapped his right rear wheel, slid back. He braked too; that was a mistake. The heavy car lost traction, sliding. In slow motion, off-balanced in a skid, it rose on its nose, ploughing up a cloud of dust. The hamper whirled away, the cloak fluttered and was gone, then the pirate car seemed to float for an instant in air, before it dropped, wheels up, out of sight over the sheer cliff. We raced alone down the slope and out onto the wooded plain toward the towers of Bar-Ponderone.

A shout went up; Owner Gope leaned forward to pound my back. "By the nine eyes of the Hill Devil!" he bellowed, "masterfully executed! The prince of pipers is a prince of drivers too! This night you'll sit by my side at the ringboard at Bar-Ponderone in the rank of a hundred-lash Chief Driver, I swear it!"

I SPENT the first day at Bar-Ponderone rubbernecking the tall buildings and keeping an eye open for Foster, on the off chance that I might pass him on the street. By sunset I was no wiser than before. Dressed in the latest in Vallonian cape and ruffles, I was sitting with my drinking buddy Cagu, Chief Bodyguard to Owner Gope, at a small table on the first terrace at the Palace of Merrymaking, Bar-Ponderone's biggest community feasting hall. It looked like a Hollywood producer's idea of a twenty-first century night club, complete with nine dance floors on five levels, indoor pools, fountains, two thousand tables, musicians, girls, noise, colored lights, plenty of booze, and food fit for an Owner. It was open to all fifty-lash-and over goodmen of the estate and to guests of equivalent rank.

Cagu was a morose-looking old cuss, but good-hearted. His face was cut and scarred from a thousand encounters with other bodyguards and his nose had been broken so often that it was invisible in profile.

"Where do you manage to get in all the fights, Cagu?" I asked him. "I've known you for three months, and I haven't seen a blow struck in anger yet."

Cagu finished off an oily greenish drink and signaled for another.

"Here." He grinned, showing me some broken front teeth. "Swell places, these big Estates, good Drgon; lotsa action."

"What do you do, get in street fights?"

"Nah. The boys show up down here, tank up, cruise around, you know."

"They start fights here in the, dining room?"

"Sure. Good crowd here; lotsa laughs."

I PICKED up my drink, raised it to Cagu—and got it in my lap as somebody jostled my arm. I looked up. A battle-scarred thug stood over me.

"Who'sa punk, Cagu?" he said in a hoarse whisper.

Cagu took a pull on a fresh drink, put the glass down, stood up, and threw a punch to the other plug-ugly's paunch. He oofed, clinched, eyed me resentfully over Cagu's shoulder. Cagu pushed him away, held him at arm's length.

"Howsa boy, Mull?" he said. "Lay offa my sidekick;

greatest little piper ina business, and a top driver too. How about a drink?"

"Sure." Mull rubbed his stomach, sat down beside me. "Ya losin' your punch, Cagu." He looked at me. "Sorry about the booze in the lap. I thought you was one of the guys." He signaled a passing waiter-slave. "Bring my friend a new suit, and a shot. Make it snappy."

"Don't the customers kind of resent it when you birds stage a heavyweight bout in the aisle?" I asked.

"Nah; we move down inta the Spot." He waved a thumb in the general direction of somewhere else. He looked me over. "Where ya been, piper? Your first time ina Palace?"

"Drgon's been travelling," said Cagu. "He's okay. Lemee tell ya the time these pirates pull one, see..."

Cagu and Mull swapped lies while I worked on my drinking. Although I hadn't learned anything on my day's looking around at Bar-Ponderone, it was still a better spot for snooping than Rath-Gallion. There were two major cities on the Estate and scores of villages. Somewhere among the population I might have better luck finding someone to talk history with...or someone who knew Foster.

"Hey!" growled Mull. "Look who's comin'."

I followed his gaze. Three thick-set thugs swaggered up to the table. One of them, a long armed gorilla at least seven feet tall, reached out, took Cagu and Mull by the backs of their necks, and cracked their skulls together. I jumped up, ducked a hoof-like fist...and saw a beautiful burst of fireworks followed by soothing darkness.

I FUMBLED in the dark with lengths of cloth entangling my legs, sat up and cracked my head—

I groaned, freed a leg from the chair rungs, groped my way out from under the table. A waiter-slave helped me up, dusted me off. The seven-foot lout lolling in a chair glanced my way, nodded.

"You shouldn't hang out with lugs like that Mull," he said. "Cagu told me you was just a piper, but the way you come outa that chair—" He shrugged, turned back to whatever he was watching.

I checked a few elbow and knee joints, worked my jaw, tried my neck: all okay.

"You the one that slugged me?" I asked.

"Huh? Yeah."

I stepped over to his chair, picked a spot, and cleared my throat. "Hey, you," I said. He turned, and I put everything I had behind a straight right to the point of the jaw. He went over, feet in the air, flipped a rail, and crashed down between two tables below. I leaned over the rail. A party of indignant tally-clerks stared up at me.

A shout went up from the floor some distance away. I looked. In a cleared circle two levels below a pair of heavy-shouldered men were slugging it out. One of them was Cagu. I watched, saw his opponent fall. Another man stepped in to take his place. I turned and made my way down to the ringside.

Cagu exchanged haymakers with two more opponents before he folded and was hauled from the ring. I propped him up in a chair, fitted a drink into his fist, and watched the boys pound each other. It was easy to see why the scarred face was the sign of their craft; there was no defensive fighting whatever. They stood toe-to-toe and hit as hard as they could, until one collapsed. It wasn't fancy, but the fans loved it. Cagu came to after a while and filled me in on the fighters' backgrounds.

"So they're all top boys," he said. "But it ain't like in the old days when I was in my prime. I could've took any three of these bums. The only one maybe I woulda had a little trouble with is Torbu."

"Which one is he?"

"He ain't down there yet; he'll show to take on the last boys on their feet."

More gladiators pushed their way to the Spot, downed drinks, pulled off gaily-patterned cloaks and weskits, and waded in.

After an hour the waiting line had dwindled away to nothing.

"Where's Torbu?"

"Maybe he didn't come tonight," I said.

"Sure, you met him; he knocked you under the table."

"Oh, him?"

"Where'd he go?"

"The last I saw he was asleep on the floor," I said.

"Hozzat?"

"I didn't much like him slugging me. I clobbered him one."

"Hey!" yelped Cagu. His face lit up. He got to his feet and floored the closest fighter, turned and laid out the other. He raised both hands above his head.

"Rath-Gallion gotta champion," he bellowed. "Rath-Gallion takes on all comers." He turned, waved to me. "Our boy, Drgon, he—"

THERE was a bellow behind me, even louder than Cagu's, I turned, saw Torbu, his hair mussed, his face purple, pushing through the crowd.

"Jussa crummy minute," he yelled. "I'm the champion around here—" He aimed a haymaker at Cagu; Cagu ducked.

"Our boy, Drgon, laid you out cold, right?" he shouted. "So now he's the champion."

"I wasn't set." Bawled Torbu. "A lucky punch."

"Come on down, Drgon," Cagu called, waving to me again. "We'll show—" Torbu turned and slammed a roundhouse right to the side of Cagu's jaw; the old fighter hit the floor hard, skidded, lay still. I got to my feet. They pulled him to the nearest table, hoisted him into a chair. I made my way down to the little clearing in the crowd. A man bending over Cagu straightened, face white. I pushed him aside, grabbed the bodyguard's wrist. There was no pulse. Cagu was dead.

Torbu stood in the center of the Spot, mouth open. "What...?" he started. I pushed between two fans, went for him. He saw me, crouched, swung out at me.

I ducked, uppercut him. He staggered back. I pressed him, threw lefts and rights to the body, ducked under his wild swings, then rocked his head left and right. He stood, knees together, eyes glazed, hands down. I measured him, right-crossed his jaw; he dropped like a log.

Panting, I looked across at Cagu. His scarred face, white as wax, was strangely altered now; it looked peaceful. I took a bottle from a waiter-slave, poured out a stiff drink, then a couple more. Somebody helped Torbu to his feet, walked him to the ringside. I had another drink. It had been a big evening. Now all I had to do was take the body home...

I went over to where Cagu was laid out on the floor. Shocked people stood around staring. Torbu was on his knees beside the body. A tear ran down his nose, dripped on Cagu's face. Torbu wiped it away with a big scarred hand.

"I'm sorry, old friend," he said. "I didn't mean it, you know I didn't."

I picked Cagu up and got him over my shoulder, and all the way to the far exit it was so quiet in the Palace of Merrymaking that I could hear my own heavy breathing.

IN the bodyguards' quarters I laid Cagu out on the bunk, then faced the dozen scowling bruisers who stared down at the still body.

"Cagu was a good man," I said. "Now he's dead. He died like an animal...for nothing."

Mull glowered at me. "You talk like we was to blame," he said. "Cagu was my compeer too."

"Whose pal was he a thousand years ago?" I snapped. "What was he—once? What were you? Vallon wasn't always like this. There was a time when every man was his own Owner—"

"Look, you ain't of the Brotherhood—" one thug started.

"So that's what you call it? But it's just another name for an old racket. A big shot sets himself up as dictator—"

"We got our Code," Mull said. "Our job is to stick up for the Owner...and that don't mean standing around listening to some japester callin' names."

"Names, hell," I snapped. "I'm talking rebellion. You boys have all the muscle and most of the guts in this organization. Why let the boss live off the fat while you murder each other for the amusement of the patrons? You had a birthright...once. But it's up to you to collect it... before more of you go the way Cagu did."

There was an angry mutter. Torbu came in, face swollen.

"Hold it, you birds," Torbu said. "What's goin' on?"

"This guy! He's talkin' revolt and treason," somebody said.

"He wants we should pull some rough stuff—on Owner Qohey hisself."

Torbu came up to me. "You're a stranger around Bar-Ponderone. Cagu said you was okay. You worked me over pretty good...and I got no hard feelin's; that's the breaks. But don't try to start no trouble here. We got our Code and our Brotherhood. We look out for each other; that's good enough for us. Owner Qohey ain't no worse than any other Owner...and by the Code, we'll stand by him!"

"Listen to me," I said. "I know the history of Vallon: I

know what you were once and what you could be again. All you have to do is take over the power. I can lead you to the ship I came here in. There are briefing rods aboard, enough to show you—"

"That's enough," Torbu broke in. He made a cabalistic sign in the air. "We ain't gettin' mixed up in no tabu ghostboats or takin' on no magicians and demons—"

"Hog wash! That tabu routine is just a gag to keep you away from the cities so you won't discover what you're missing—"

"I don't wanna hafta take you to the Greymen, Drgon," Torbu growled. "Leave it lay."

"These cities," I ploughed on. "They're standing there, empty, as perfect as the day they were built. And you live in these fleabitten quarters, jammed inside the town walls, so the Greymen and renegades won't get you."

"You wanna runs things here?" Mull put in. "Go see Qohey."

"Let's all go see Qohey!" I said.

"That's something you'll have to do alone, "said Torbu. "You better move on, Drgon. I ain't turnin' you in; I know how you felt about Cagu gettin' killed and all—but don't push it too far."

I knew I was licked. They were as stubborn as a team of mules—and just about as smart.

TORBU motioned; I followed him outside.

"You wanna turn things upside-down, don't you? I know how it is; you ain't the first guy to get ideas. We can't help you. But we got a legend: someday the Rthr will come back...and then the Good Time will come back too."

"What's the Rthr?" I said.

"Kinda like a big-shot Owner. There ain't no Rthr now. But a long time ago, back when our first lives started, there

was a Rthr that was Owner of all Vallon, and everybody lived
high, and had all their lives...it's kind of like a hope we got—
that's what we're waitin' for through all our lives."

"Okay," I said. "Dream on, big boy. And while you're
treasuring your rosy dreams you'll get your brains kicked out,
like Cagu." I turned away.

"Listen, Drgon. It's no good buckin' the system: it's too
big for one guy...or even a bunch of guys...but—"

I looked up. "Yeah?"

"...if you gotta stick your neck out—see Owner Gope."
Abruptly Torbu turned and pushed back through the door.

See Owner Gope, huh? Okay, what did I have to lose?

I STOOD in the middle of the deep-pile carpet in Gope's
suite, trying to keep my temper hot enough to supply the gall
I needed to bust in on an Owner in the middle of the night.
He sat in his ceremonial chair and stared at me impassively.

"With your help or without it," I said, "I'm going to find
the answers."

"Yes, good Drgon," he said, not bellowing for once. "I
understand. But there are matters you don't understand."

"I understand too much," I snapped. "Do you remember
Cagu? Maybe you remember him as a newman, young,
handsome, like a god out of some old legend? You've seen
him live his life. Was it a good life? Did the promise of
youth ever get paid off? And what about yourself? Don't
you ever wonder what you might have been...back in the
Good Time?"

"Who are you?" asked Gope, his eyes fixed on mine.
"You speak Old Vallonian, you rake up the forbidden
knowledge, and challenge the very Powers..." He got to his
feet. "I could have you immured, Drgon. I could hand you
to the Greymen, for a fate I shudder to name." He turned
and walked the length of the room restlessly, then turned

back to me and stopped.

"Matters stand ill with this fair world," he said. "Legend tells us that once men lived as the High Gods on Vallon. There was a mighty Owner, Rthr of all Vallon. It is whispered that he will come again—"

"Your legends are all true. You can take my word for that! But that doesn't mean some supernatural sugar daddy is going to come along and bail you out. And don't get the idea I think I'm the fabled answer to prayers. All I mean is that once upon a time Vallon was a good place to live and it could be again. Your cities and roads and ships are still here, intact. But nobody knows how to run them and you're all afraid to try. Who scared you off? What broke down the memory recording system? Why can't we all go to Okk-Hamiloth and use the Archives to give everybody back what he's lost—"

"These are dread words," said Gope.

"There must be somebody behind it. Or there was once. Who is he?"

GOPE thought. "There is one man pre-eminent among us: the Great Owner, Owner of Owners: Ommodurad by name. Where he dwells I know not. This is a secret possessed only by his intimates."

"What does he look like? How do I get to see him?"

Gope shook his head. "I have seen him but once, closely cowled. He is a tall man, and silent. 'Tis said—" Gope lowered his voice, "—by his black arts he possesses all his lives. An aura of dread hangs all about him—"

"Never mind that jazz," I said. "How can I get close to him?"

"There are those Owners who are his confidants," said Gope, "his trusted agents. It is through them that we small Owners learn of his will."

"Can we enlist one of them?"

"Never. They are bound to him by ties of darkness, spells, and incantations."

"I'm a fast man with a pair of loaded dice myself. It's all done with mirrors. Let's stick to the point. How can I work into a spot with one of these big shots?"

"Nothing easier. A driver and piper of such skills as your own can claim whatever place he chooses."

"Now about bodyguarding? Suppose I could take a heavy named Torbu; would that set me in better with a new Owner?"

"Such is no place for a man of your abilities, good Drgon," Gope exclaimed. "True, 'tis a place most close to an Owner, but there is much danger in it. The challenge involves the most bloody hand-to-hand combat, second only to the rigors of a challenge to an Owner himself."

"What's that?" I snapped. "Challenge an Owner?"

"Be calm, good Drgon," said Gope, staring at me incredulously. "No common man with his wits about him will challenge an Owner. He is a warrior trained in the skills of battle. None less than another such may hope to prevail."

I smacked my fist into my palm. "I should have thought of this sooner! The cooks cook for their places, the pipers pipe...and the best man wins. It figures that the Owners would use the same system. But what's the procedure? How do you get your chance to prove who can own the best?"

"It is a contest with naked steel. It is the measure and glory of an Owner that he alone stands ready to prove his quality against the peril of death itself." Gope drew himself up with pride.

"What Owner can I challenge? How do I go about it? What's the procedure?"

"Give up this course, good Drgon—"

"Where's the nearest buddy of the Big Owner?"

Gope threw up his hands. "Here, at Bar-Ponderone. Owner Qohey. But—"

"And how do I call his bluff?" I asked.

Gope put a hand on my shoulder. "It is no bluff, good Drgon. It is long now since last Owner Qohey stood to his blade to protect his place, but you may be sure he has lost none of his skill. Thus it was he won his way to Bar-Ponderone, while lesser knights, such as myself, contented themselves with meaner fiefs."

"I'm not bluffing either, noble Gope," I said, stretching a point. "I was no harness-maker in the Good Time."

Gope sat down heavily, raised his hands, and let them fall. "If I tell you not, another will. But I will not soon find another piper of your worth."

## CHAPTER FIFTEEN

GAUDY hangings of purple cut the light of the sun to a rich gloom in the enormous, high-vaulted Audience Hall. A rustling murmur was audible in the room as uneasy courtiers and supplicants fidgeted, waiting for the appearance of the Owner.

It had been two months since Gope had explained to me how a formal challenge to an Owner was conducted, and, as he pointed out, this was the only kind of challenge that would help. If I waylaid the man and cut him down, even in a fair fight, his bodyguards would repay the favor before I could establish the claim that I was their legitimate new boss.

I had spent three hours every day in the armory at Rath-Gallion, trading buffets with Gope and a couple of the bodyguards. The thirty-pound slab of edged steel had felt right at home in my hand that first day—for about a minute. I had the borrowed knowledge to give me all the technique I needed, but the muscle power for putting the knowledge into practice was another matter. After five minutes I was slumped against the wall, gulping air, while Gope whistled his sticker around my head and talked.

"You laid on like no piper, good Drgon. Yet have you much to learn in the matter of endurance."

After surviving two months of Gope's training I felt ready for anything. Gope had warned me that Owner Qohey was a big fellow, but that didn't bother me. The bigger they came, the bigger the target...

There was a murmur in a different key in the Audience Hall and tall gilt doors opened at the far side of the room. A couple of liveried flunkies scampered into view, then a seven-foot man-eater stalked into the hall, made his way to the dais, turned to face the crowd...

He was enormous: his neck was as thick as my thigh, his features chipped out of granite, the grey variety. He threw back his brilliant purple cloak from his shoulders and reached out for the ceremonial sword one of the flunkies was struggling with; his arm was like an oak root. He took the sword with its sheath, sat down, and stood it between his feet his arms folded on top.

WHO has a grievance?" he spoke. The voice reverberated like the old Wurlitzer at the Rialto back home.

This was my cue. There he was, just asking for it. All I had to do was speak up. Owner Qohey would gladly oblige me.

I cleared my throat with a thin squeak, and edged forward,

not very far.

"I have one little item—" I started.

Nobody was listening. Up front a big fellow in a black toga was pushing through the crowd. Everybody turned to stare at him, there was a craning of necks. The crowd drew back from the dais leaving an opening. The man in black stepped into the clear, flung back the flapping garment from his right arm, and whipped out a long polished length of razor-edged iron. It was beginning to look like somebody had beaten me to the punch.

The newcomer stood there in front of Qohey with the naked blade making all the threat that was needed. Qohey stared at him for a long moment, then stood, gestured to a flunky. The flunky turned, cleared his throat.

"The place of Bar-Ponderone has been claimed!" he recited in a shrill voice. "Let the issue be joined!" He skittered out of the way and Qohey rose, threw aside his purple cloak and cowl, and stepped down. I pushed forward to get a better look.

The challenger in black tossed his loose garment aside, stood facing Qohey in a skin-tight jerkin and hose; heavy moccasins of soft leather were laced up the calf. He was magnificently muscled but Qohey was bigger.

Qohey unsheathed his fancy iron and whirled it up overhead, made a few practice swipes. He handled it like it was a lady's putter. I felt sorry for the smaller man, who was just standing, watching him. He really didn't have a chance.

I had got through to the fore rank by now. The challenger turned and I saw his face. I stopped dead, while fire bells clanged in my head.

The man in black was Foster.

IN dead silence Qohey and Foster squared off, touched their sword points to the floor in some kind of salute...and

Qohey's slicer whipped up in a vicious cut. Foster leaned aside, just far enough, then countered with a flick that made Qohey jump back. I let out a long breath and tried swallowing.

Qohey's blade flashed, cutting at Foster's head. Foster hardly moved. Almost effortlessly, it seemed, he interposed his heavy weapon between the attacking steel and himself. Clash, clang! Qohey hacked and chopped...and Foster played with him. Then Foster's arm flashed out and there was blood on Qohey's wrist. A gasp went up from the crowd. Now Foster took a step forward, struck...and faltered! In an instant Qohey was on him and the two men were locked, chest to chest. For a moment Foster held, then Qohey's weight told, and Foster reeled back. He tried to bring up the sword, seemed to struggle, then Qohey lashed out again. Foster twisted, took the blow awkwardly just above the hand guard, stumbled...and fell.

Qohey leaped to him, raised the sword—

I hauled mine half way out of its sheath and pushed forward.

"Let the man be put away from my sight," rumbled Qohey. He lowered his immense sword, turned, pushed aside a flunky who had bustled up with a wad of bandages. As he strode from the room a swarm of bodyguards fanned out between the crowd and Foster. I could see him clumsily struggling to rise, then I was shoved back, still craning for a glimpse. There was something wrong here; Foster had acted like a man suddenly half-paralyzed. Had Qohey doped him in some way?

The cordon stopped pushing. I tugged at the arm of the bodyguard beside me. "What's to be the fate of the man?" I asked.

"They're gonna immure him."

"You mean wall him up?"

"Yeah. Just a peep hole to pass chow in every day...so's he don't starve, see?"

"How long—?"

"He'll last; don't worry. After the Change, Owner Qohey's got a newman—"

"Shut up," another bruiser said.

THE crowd was slowly thinning. The bodyguards were relaxing, standing in pairs talking. Two servants moved about where the fight had taken place, making mystical motions in the air above the floor. I edged forward, watching them. They seemed to be plucking imaginary flowers.

I moved even farther forward to take a closer look, then saw a tiny glint... A servant hurried across, made gestures. I pushed him aside, groped...and my fingers encountered a delicate filament of wire. I pulled it in, swept up more. The servants had stopped and stood watching me, muttering. The whole area of the combat was covered with the invisible wires, looping up in coils two feet high.

No wonder Foster had stumbled, had trouble raising his sword. He had been netted, encased in a mesh of incredibly fine tough wire...and in the dim light even the crowd twenty feet away hadn't seen it. I put my hand on my sword hilt, chewed my lower lip. I had found Foster...but it wouldn't do me—or Vallon—much good. He was on his way to the dungeons, to be walled up until the next Change. And it would be three months before I could legally make another try for Qohey's place. I would have to spend that time working on my swordplay, and hope Foster could hold out. Maybe I could sneak a message—

A heavy blow on the back sent me spinning. Four bodyguards moved to ring me in, clubs in hand. They were strangers to me, but across the room I saw Torbu looming, looking my way...

"I saw him; he started to pull that fancy sword," said one of the guards.

"He was asking me questions—"

"Unbuckle it and drop it," another ordered me. "Don't try anything!"

"What's this all about?" I said. "I have a right to wear a Ceremonial Sword at an Audience—"

"Move in, boys!" The four men stepped toward me, the clubs came up. I warded off a smashing blow with my left arm, took a blinding crack across the face, felt myself going down—another blow, and another: all killing ones...

Then I was aware of being dragged, endlessly, of voices barking sharp questions, of pain... After a long time it was dark, and silent, and I slept.

I GROANED and the sound was dead, muffled. I put out a hand and touched stone on my right. My left elbow touched stone. I made an instinctive move to sit up and smacked my head against more stone. My new room was confining. I felt my face...and winced at the touch. The bridge of my nose felt different: it was lower than it used to be, in spite of the swelling. I lay back and traced the pattern of pain. There was the nose—smashed flat—with secondary aches around the eyes. They'd be beautiful shiners, if I could see them. Now the left arm: it was curled close to my side and when I moved it I saw why: it wasn't broken, but the shoulder wasn't right, and there was a deep bruise above the elbow. My knees and shin, as far as I could reach, were caked with dried blood. That figured: I remembered being dragged.

I tried deep-breathing; my chest seemed to be okay. My hands worked. My teeth were in place. Maybe I wasn't as sick as I felt.

But where the hell was I? The floor was hard, cold. I

needed a big soft bed and a little soft nurse and a hot meal and a cold drink...

Foster! I cracked my head again and flopped back, groaned some more. It still sounded pretty dead.

I swallowed, licked my lips, felt a nice split that ran down to the bristles. I had attended the Audience clean-shaven. Quite a few hours have passed since then. They had taken Foster away to immure him, sombody said. Then the guards had tapped me, worked me over—

Immured! I got a third crack on the head. Suddenly it was hard to breathe. I was walled up, sealed away from the light, buried under the foundations of the giant towers of Bar-Ponderone, I felt their crushing weight...

I forced myself to relax, breathe deep. Being immured wasn't the same as being buried alive—not exactly. This was the method these latter-day Vallonians had figured out to effectively end a man's life...without ending all his lives. They figured to keep me neatly packaged here until my next Change, thus acquiring another healthy newman for the kitchen or the stables. They didn't know the only Change that would happen to me was death.

They'd have to feed me; that meant a hole. I ran my fingers along the rough stone, found an eight-inch square opening on the left wall, just under the ceiling. I reached through it, felt nothing but the solidness of its thick sides. How far along the other open end was I had no way of determining.

I was feeling dizzy. I lay back and tried to think, but everything remained fuzzy.

I WAS awake again. There had been a sound. I moved, and felt something hit my chest.

I groped for it; it was a small loaf of hard bread. I heard

the sound again and a second object thumped against me.

"Hey!" I yelled, "listen to me! I'll die in here. I'm not like the rest of you; I won't go through a Change. I'll rot here until I die. Do you hear me...?"

I listened. The silence was absolute.

"Answer me!" I screamed. "You're making a mistake...!"

I gave up when my throat got raw. I felt for the other item that had been pushed in to me. It was a water bottle made of tough plastic. I fumbled the cap off, took a swallow. It wasn't good. I tried the bread; it was tough, tasteless. I lay and chewed and thought. As a world-saver I was a bust. I had come a long long way and now I was going to die in this reeking hole. I had a sudden vision of steaks uneaten, wines undrunk, girls unhad, and life unlived. And then I had another thought: if I never had them was it going to be because I hadn't tried? Abruptly I was planning. I would keep calm and use my head. I wouldn't wear myself out with screams and struggles. I'd figure the angles, use everything I had to make the best try I could.

First, to explore the tomb-cell. It hurt to move but that didn't matter. I felt over the walls, estimating size. My chamber was three feet wide, two feet high, and seven feet long. The walls were relatively smooth, except for a few mortal joints. The stones were big: eighteen inches or so by a couple of feet. I scratched at the mortar; it was rock hard.

I wondered how they'd gotten me in. Some of the stones must be newly placed...or else there was a door. I couldn't feel anything as far as my hands would reach. Maybe at the other end...

I tried to twist around: no go. The people who had built the cage knew just how to dimension it to keep the occupant oriented the way they wanted him. He was supposed to just lie quietly and wait for the bread and water to fall through the hole above his chest.

That was reason enough to change positions. If they wanted me to stay put I'd at least have the pleasure of defying the rules. And there just might be a reason why they didn't want me moving around.

I turned on my side, pulled my legs up, hugged them to my chest, worked my way down...and jammed. My skinned knees and shins didn't help any. I inched them higher, wincing at the pain, then braced my hands against the floor and roof and with all my strength forced my torso toward my feet...

Still no go. The rough stone was shredding my back. I moved my knees apart; that eased the pressure a little. I made another inch.

I RESTED, tried to get some air. It wasn't easy: my chest was crushed between my thighs and the stone wall at my back. I breathed shallowly, wondering whether I should go back or try to push on. I tried to move my legs; they didn't like the idea. I might as well go on. It would be no fun either way and if I waited I'd stiffen up, while inactivity and no food and loss of blood would weaken me further every moment. I wouldn't do better next time—not even as well. This was the time. Now.

I set myself, pushed again, I didn't move. I pushed harder, scraping my palms raw against the stone. I was stuck—good. I went limp suddenly. Then I panicked, in the grip of claustrophobia. I snarled, rammed my hands hard against the floor and wall, and heaved—and felt my lacerated back slip along the stone, sliding on a lubricating film of blood. I pushed again, my back curved, doubled; my knees were forced up beside my ears. I couldn't breathe at all now and my spine was breaking. It didn't matter. I might as well break it, rip off all the hide, bleed to death; I had nothing to lose. I shoved again, felt the back of my head grate; my neck bent, creaking…then I was through, stretching out to flop on my back gasping, my head where my feet had been. Score one for our side.

IT took a long time to get my breath back and sort out my various abrasions. My back was worst, then my legs and hands. There was a messy spot on the back of my head and sharp pains shot down my spine, and I was getting tired of breathing through my mouth instead of my smashed nose. Other than that I'd never felt better in my life. I had plenty of room to relax in, I could breathe. All I had to do was rest, and after a while they'd drop some more nice bread and water in to me…

I shook myself awake. There was something about the absolute darkness and silence that made my mind want to curl up and sleep, but there was no time for that. If there had been a stone freshly set in mortar to seal the chamber after I had been stuffed inside, this was the time to find it—before it set too hard. I ran my hands over the wall, found the joints. The mortar was dry and hard in the first, but the next was different. Under my fingernail soft mortar crumbled away. I traced the joint; it ran around a twelve-by-eighteen-inch stone. I raised myself on my elbow, settled down to scratching at it.

Half an hour later I had ten bloody fingertips and a half-inch groove cut around the stone. It was slow work, and I couldn't go much farther without a tool of some sort. I felt for the water bottle, took off the cap, tried to crush it. It wouldn't crush. There was nothing else in the cell.

Maybe the stone would move, mortar and all, if I shoved hard enough. I set my feet against the end wall, my hands against the block and strained until the blood roared in my ears. No use.

I was lying there, just thinking about it, when I became

aware of something. It wasn't a noise exactly. It was more like a fourth-dimensional sound heard inside the brain...or the memory of one.

But my next sensation was perfectly real. I felt four little feet walking gravely up my chest toward my chin

It was the cat, Itzenca.

## CHAPTER SIXTEEN

FOR a while I toyed with the idea of just chalking it up as a miracle. Then I decided it would be a nice problem in probabilities. It had been seven months since we had parted company on the pink terrace at Okk-Hamiloth. Where would I have gone if I had been a cat? And how could I have found me—my old pal from Earth?

Itzenca exhaled a snuffle in my ear.

"Come to think of it, the stink is pretty strong, isn't it? I guess there's nobody on Vallon with quite the same heady fragrance. And what with the close quarters here, the concentration of sweat, blood, and you-name-it must be pretty penetrating."

Itz didn't seem to care. She marched around my head and back again, now and then laid a tentative paw on my nose or chin, and kept up a steady rumbling purr. The feeling of affection I had for that cat right then was close to being one of my life's grand passions. I couldn't keep my hands off her. They roamed over her scrawny frame, fingered again the khaffite collar I had whiled away an hour in fashioning for her aboard the lifeboat—

My head hit the stone wall with a crash I didn't even notice. In ten seconds I had released the collar clasp, pulled the collar from Itzenca's neck, thumbed the stiff khaffite out into a blade about ten inches long, and was scraping at the mortar beyond my head at fever heat.

They had fed me three times by the time the groove was nine inches deep on all sides of the block, and the mortar had hardened. But I was nearly through, I figured. I took a rest, then made another try at loosening the block. I stuck the blade in the slot, levered gently at the stone. If it was only supported on one edge now, as it would be if it were a little less than a foot thick, it should be about ready to go. I couldn't tell.

I put down my scraper, got in position, and pushed. I wasn't as strong as I had been; there wasn't much force in the push. Again I rested and again I tried. Maybe there was only a thin crust of mortar still holding; maybe one more ounce of pressure would do it. I took a deep breath, strained...and felt the block shift minutely.

Now! I heaved again, teeth gritted, drew back my feet, and thrust hard. The stone slid out with a grating sound, dropped half an inch. I paused to listen: all quiet. I shoved again, and the stone dropped with a heavy thud to the floor outside. With no loss of time I pushed through behind it, felt a breath of cooler air, got my shoulders free, pulled my legs through...and stood, for the first time in how many days...

I HAD already figured my next move. As soon as Itzenca had stepped out I reached back in, groped for the water bottle, the dry crusts I had been saving, and the wad of bread paste I had made up. I reached a second time for a handful of the powdered mortar I had produced, then lifted the stone. I settled it in place, using the hard bread as supports, then packed the open joint with gummy bread. I dusted it over with dry mortar, then carefully swept up the debris—as well as I could in the total darkness. The bread-and-water man would have a light and he was due in half an hour or so—as closely as I had been able to estimate the time of his regular round. I didn't want him to see anything out of the ordinary. I was counting on finding Foster filed away somewhere in the stacks, and I'd need time to try to release him.

I moved along the corridor, counting my steps, one hand full of bread crumbs and stone dust, the other feeling the wall. There were narrow side branches every few feet; the access ways to the feeding holes. Forty-one paces from my slot I came to a wooden door. It wasn't locked, but I didn't open it. I wasn't ready to use it yet.

I went back, passed my hole, continued nine paces to a blank wall. Then I tried the side branches. They were all seven-foot stubs, dead ends; each had the eight-inch holes on either side. I called Foster's name softly at each hole...but there was no answer. I heard no signs of life, no yells or heavy breathing. Was I the only one here? That wasn't what I had figured on. Foster had to be in one of these delightful bedrooms. I had come across the universe to see him and I wasn't going to leave Bar-Ponderone without him.

It was time to get ready for the bread man. I groped my way into one of the side branches; Itzenca at my heels. With half a year's experience at dodging humans behind her, she could be trusted not to show at the crucial moment, I figured. I had just jettisoned my handful of trash in the back-most corner of the passage when there was a soft grating sound from the door. I flattened myself against the wall.

A light splashed on the floor; it must have been dim but seemed to my eyes like the blaze of noon. Soft footsteps sounded. I held my breath. A man in bodyguard's trappings, basket in hand. moved past the entry of the branch where I stood, went on. I breathed again. Now all I had to do was keep an eye on the feeder, watch where he stopped. I stepped to the corridor, risked a glance, saw him entering a branch farther down the corridor. As he disappeared I made it three branches farther along, ducked out of sight.

I heard him coming back. I flattened myself. He went by me, opened the door. It closed behind him. Darkness, silence and despair settled down once more.

The bread man had stopped at one cell only—mine. Foster wasn't there.

IT was a long wait for the next feeding but I put the time to use. First I had a good nap; I hadn't been getting my rest while I scratched my way out of my nest. I woke up feeling better and started thinking about the next move. The door creaked, and I did a fast fade down a side branch. The guard shuffled into view; now was the time. I moved out—quietly, I thought, and he whirled, dropped the load and bottle, and fumbled at his club hilt. I didn't have a club to slow me down. I went at him, threw a beautiful right, square to the mouth. He went over backwards, with me on top. I heard his head hit with a sound like a length of rubber hose slapping a grapefruit. He didn't move.

I pulled the clothes off him, struggled into them. They didn't fit too well and they probably smelled gamey to anybody who hadn't spent a week where I had, but details like these didn't count anymore. I tore his sash into strips and tied him. He wasn't dead—quite, but I had reason to know that any yelling he did was unlikely to attract much attention. I hoped he'd enjoy the rest and quiet until the next feeding time. By then I expected to be long gone. I lifted the door open and stepped out into a dimly lit corridor.

With Itzenca abreast of me I moved along in absolute stillness, passed a side corridor, came to a heavy door; locked.

We retraced our steps, went down the side hall, found a flight of worn steps, followed them up two flights, and emerged in a dark room. A line of light showed around a door. I went to it, peered through the crack. Two men in stained kitchen-slave tunics fussed over a boiling cauldron. I pushed through the door.

The two looked up, startled. I rounded a littered table, grabbed up a heavy soup ladle, and skulled the nearest cook just as he opened up to yell. The other one, a big fellow, went for a cleaver. I caught him in two jumps, laid him out cold beside his pal.

I found an apron, ripped it up, and tied and gagged the two slaves, then hauled them into a storeroom.

I came back into the kitchen. It was silent now. The room reeked of sour soup. A stack of unpleasantly familiar loaves stood by the oven. I gave them a kick that collapsed the pile as I passed to pick up a knife. I hacked tough slices from a cold haunch of Vallonian mutton, threw one to Itzenca across the table, and sat and gnawed the meat while I tried to think through my plans.

OWNER Qohey was a big man to tackle but he was the one with the answers. If I could make my way to his apartment and if I wasn't stopped before I'd forced the truth out of him, then I might get to Foster and tell him that if he had the memory playback machine I had the memory, if it hadn't been filched from the bottom of a knapsack aboard a lifeboat parked at Okk-Hamiloth.

Four 'if's' and a 'might'—but it was something to shoot at. My first move would be to locate Qohey's quarters, somewhere in the Palace, and get inside. My bodyguard's outfit was as good a disguise as any for the attempt.

I finished off my share of the meat and got to my feet. I'd have to find a place to clean myself up, shave—

The rear door banged open and two bodyguards came through it, talking loudly, laughing.

"Hey, cook! Set out meat and wine for—"

The heavy in the lead stopped short, gaping at me. I gaped back. It was Torbu.

"Drgon! How did you..." He trailed off.

The other bodyguard came past him, looked me over. "You're no Brother of the Guard—" he started.

I reached for the cleaver the kitchen-slave had left on the table, backed against a tall wall cupboard. The bodyguard unlimbered his club.

"Hold it, Blon," said Torbu. "Drgon's okay." He looked at me. "I kind of figured you for done-for, Drgon. The boys worked you over pretty good."

"Yeah," I returned, "and thanks for your help in stopping it. You claim to believe in the system around here. You think it's a great life, all fair play and no holds barred and plenty of goodies for the winner. I know, it was tough about Cagu, but that's life, isn't it? But what about the business I saw in the Audience Hall? You guys try not to think about that angle, is that it?"

"It was the Owner's orders," said Blon. "What was I gonna do, tell him—?"

"Never mind," I said. "I'll tell him myself. That's all I want: just a short interview with the Owner—minus the wire nets."

"Wow..." drawled Torbu; "yeah, that'd be a bout." He turned to Blon. "This guy's got a punch, Blon. He don't look so hot but he could swap buffets with the Fire Drgon he's named after. If he's that good with a long blade—"

"Just lend me one," I said, "and show me the way to his apartment."

"I didn't like the capers with the wires, neither did most of the boys. We're Brothers of the Guard," said Torbu. "We ain't got much but we got our Code. It don't say nothing about wires. If we don't back up our oath to the Brotherhood we ain't no better than slaves." He turned to me. "Come on, Drgon. We'll take you to the Guardroom so you can clean up and put on a good blade. If you're gonna lose all your lives at once, you wanna do it right."

TORBU watched as the boys belted and strapped me into a guardsman's fighting outfit. I had made him uneasy, maybe even started him thinking.

I felt better in the clean trappings of tough leather and steel. Torbu led the way and fifteen bodyguards followed, like a herd of Trolls. We stopped before a great double door. Two guards in dress purple sauntered over to see what it was all about. Torbu clued them in. They hesitated, looked us over...

"We're goin' in, rookie," said Torbu. "Open up." They did.

I pushed past Torbu into a room whose splendor made Gope's state apartment look like a four-dollar motel. Bright Cintelight streamed through tall windows, showed me a wide bed and somebody in it. I went to it, grabbed the bedclothes, and hauled them to the floor. Owner Qohey sat up slowly—seven feet of muscle. He looked at me, glanced past me to the foremost of my escort...

He was out of bed like a tiger coming straight for me. There was no time to fumble with the sword. I went to meet him, threw all my weight into a right haymaker and felt it connect. I plunged past, whirled.

Qohey was staggering...but still on his feet. I had hit him with everything I had, nearly broken my fist...and he was still standing. I couldn't let him rest. I was after him, slammed a hard punch to the kidneys, caught him across the jaw as he turned, drove a left and right into his stomach—

A girder fell from the top of the Golden Gate Bridge and shattered every bone in my body. There was a booming like heavy surf, and I was floating in it, dead. Then I was in Hell, being prodded by red-hot tridents... I blinked my eyes. The roaring was fading now. I saw Qohey, leaning against the foot of the bed, breathing heavily. I had to get him.

I got my feet under me, stood up. My chest was caved in and my left arm belonged to somebody else. Okay; I still had my right. I made it over to Qohey, maneuvered into position. He didn't look at me; he seemed to be having trouble breathing; those gut punches had gotten to him. I picked a spot just behind the right ear, reared back, and threw a trip-hammer punch with my shoulder and legs behind it. I felt the jaw go. Qohey jumped the footboard and piled onto the floor like a hundred car freight hitting an open switch. I sat down on the edge of the bed and sucked in air and tried to ignore the whirling lights that were closing in.

AFTER awhile I noticed Torbu standing in front of me with the cat under one arm. Both of them were grinning at me. "Any orders, Owner Drgon?"

I found my voice. "Wake him up and prop him in a chair. I want to talk to him."

Ex-Owner Qohey didn't much like the idea but after Torbu and a couple of the other strong-arm lads had explained the situation to him in sign language he decided to co-operate.

"Get off his head, Mull," Torbu said. "And untwist that rope, Blon. Owner Drgon wants him in a conversational mood."

Qohey was looking at me now, eyes wild. He grunted something, but was having trouble talking around his broken jaw.

"The fellow in black," I said: "the one who claimed your

place as Owner. You netted him and had your bully boys haul him off somewhere. I want to know where."

Qohey grunted again.

"Hit him, Torbu," I said. "It will help his enunciations." Torbu kicked the former Owner in the shin. Qohey jumped and glowered at him.

"Call off your dogs," he mumbled. "You'll not find the upstart you seek here."

"Why not?"

"I sent him away."

"Where?"

"To that place from which you and your turncoat crew will never fetch him back."

"Be more specific."

Qohey spat.

I took out the needle-pointed knife I was wearing as part of my get-up. I put the point against Qohey's throat and pushed gently until a trickle of crimson ran down the thick neck.

"Talk," I said quietly, "or I'll cut your throat myself."

Qohey had shrunk back as far as he could in the heavy chair.

"Seek him then, assassin," he sneered. "Seek him in the dungeons of the Owner of Owners."

"Keep talking," I prompted.

"The Great Owner commanded that the slave be brought to him...at the Palace of Sapphires by the Shallow Sea."

"Has this Owners' Owner got a name?"

"Lord Ommodurad," Qohey's voice grated out.

"When did he go?"

"Yesterday."

"You know this Sapphire Palace, Torbu?"

"Sure, but the place is tabu; it's crawlin' with demons and warlocks. The word is, there's a curse on the—"

"Then I'll go in alone," I said. I put the knife away. "But first I've got a call to make at the spaceport at Okk-Hamiloth."

"Sure, Owner Drgon. The port's easy. Some say it's kind of haunted too but that's just a gag; the Greymen hang out there."

"We can take care of the Greymen," I said. "Get fifty of your best men together and line up some air-cars. I want the outfit ready to move in half an' hour."

"What about this chiseller?" asked Torbu.

"Seal him up until I get back. If I don't make it, I know he'll understand."

## CHAPTER SEVENTEEN

IT was not quite dawn when my task force settled down on the smooth landing pad beside the lifeboat that had brought me to Vallon. It stood as I had left it seven earth-months before: the port open, the access ladder extended, the interior lights lit. There weren't any spooks aboard but they had kept visitors away as effectively as if there had been. Even the Greymen didn't mess with ghostboats. Somebody had done a thorough job of indoctrination on Vallon.

Itzenca scampered up the ladder and had disappeared inside the boat by the time I took the first rung. The guards gawked from below as I stepped into the softly lit lounge. The black-and-gold banded cylinder that was Foster's memory lay in the bag where I had left it, and with it was the other, plain one. Somewhere in Okk-Hamiloth must be the machine that would give these meaning. Together, Foster and I would find it.

I found the .38 automatic lying where I had left it. I picked up the worn belt, strapped it around me. My Vallonian career to date suggested it would be a bright idea to bring it along. The Vallonians had never developed any personal armament to equal it. In a society of immortals knives were considered lethal enough for all ordinary purposes.

"Come on, cat," I said. "There's nothing more here we need."

Back on the ramp, I beckoned my platoon leaders over.

"I'm going to the Sapphire Palace," I said. "Anybody that doesn't want to go can check out now. Pass the word."

Torbu stood silent for a long moment, staring straight ahead.

"I don't like it much, Owner," he said. "But I'll go. And so will the rest of 'em."

"There'll be no backing out, once we shove off," I said. "And by the way—" I jacked a round into the chamber of the pistol, raised it, and fired the shot into the air. They all jumped. "If you ever hear that sound, come a-running."

The men nodded, turned to their cars. I picked up the cat and piled into the lead vehicle next to Torbu.

"It's a half-hour run," he said. "We might run into a little Greyman action on the way. We can handle 'em."

We lifted, swung to the east, barreled along at low altitude.

"What do we do when we get there, boss?" said Torbu.

"We play it by ear. Let's see how far we can get on pure gall before Ommodurad drops the hanky."

THE palace lay below us, rearing blue towers to the twilit sky like a royal residence in the Munchkin country. Beyond it, sunset colors reflected from the silky surface of the Shallow Sea. The timeless stones and still waters looked much as they had when Foster set out to lose his identity on Earth, three thousand years before. But its magnificence was lost on these people. The hulking crew around me never paused to wonder about the marvels wrought by their immortal ancestors—themselves—; stolidly they lived their feudal lives in dismal contrast with the monuments all about them.

We were dropping toward the wide lawns now and still no opposition showed itself. Then the towering blue spires were looming over us, and we saw men forming up behind the blue-stained steel gates of the Great Pavilion.

"A reception committee," I said. "Hold tight, fellas. Don't start anything. The further in we get peaceably the less that leaves to do the hard way."

The cars settled down gently, well grouped, and Torbu and I climbed out. As quickly as the other boats disgorged their men, ranks were closed, and we moved off toward the gates. Itzenca, as mascot, brought up the rear. Still no excitement, no rush by the Palace guards. Had too many centuries of calm made them lackadaisical, or did Ommodurad use some other brand of visitor-repellent we couldn't see from here?

We made it to the gate...and it opened.

"In we go," I said, "but be ready..."

The uniformed men inside the compound, obviously chosen for their beef content, kept their distance, looked at us queryingly. We pulled up on a broad blue-paved drive and waited for the next move.

IT was a long five minutes before a hard case in a beetle-- backed carapace or armor and a puffy pink cape bustled down the palace steps and came up to us.

"Who comes in force to the Sapphire Palace?" he demanded, glancing past me at my teammates.

"I'm Owner Drgon, fellow," I barked. "These are my honor guard. What provincial welcome is this, from the Great Owner to a loyal liege-man?"

That punctured his pomposity a little. He apologized—in a halfhearted way, mumbled something about arrangements, and beckoned over a couple of sidemen. One of them came over and spoke to Torbu, who looked my way, hand on dagger hilt.

"What's this?" I said. "Where I go, my men go."

"There is the matter of caste," said my pink-caped greeter. "Packs of retainers are not ushered *en masse* into the presence of Lord Ommodurad, Owner of Owners."

I thought that one over and failed to come up with a plausible loop-hole.

"Okay, Torbu," I said. "Keep the boys together and behave yourselves. I'll see you in an hour. Oh, and see that Itzenca gets made comfy."

The beetle man snapped a few orders, then waved me toward the palace with the slightest bow I ever saw. A six-man guard kept me company up the steps and into the Great Pavilion.

I guess I expected the usual velvet-draped audience chamber or barbarically splendid Hall, complete with pipers, fools, and ceremonial guards. What I got was an office, about sixteen by eighteen, blue-carpeted and tasteful...but bare-looking. I stopped in front of a block of blue-veined grey marble with a couple of quill pens in a crystal holder and, underneath, leg room for a behemoth, who was sitting behind the desk.

He got to his feet with all the ponderous mass of Nero Wolfe but a lot more agility and grace. "You wish?" he rumbled.

"I'm Owner Drgon, ah...Great Owner," I said. I'd planned to give my host the friendly-but-dumb routine. I was going to find the second part of the act easy. There was something about Ommodurad that made me feel like a mouse who'd just changed his mind about the cheese. Qohey had been big, but this guy could crush skulls as most men pinch peanut hulls, and in his eyes was the kind of remote look that came of three millennia of not even having to mention the power he asserted.

"You ignore superstition," observed the Big Owner. He didn't waste many words, it seemed. Gope had said he was the silent type. It wasn't a bad lead; I decided to follow it.

"Don't believe in 'em," I said.

"To your business then," he continued. "Why?"

"Just been chosen Owner at Bar-Ponderone," I said. "Felt it was only fitting that I come and do obeisance before Your Grace."

"That expression is not used."

"Oh." This fellow had a disconcerting way of not getting sucked in. "Lord Ommodurad?"

HE nodded just perceptibly, then turned to the foremost of the herd who had brought me in. "Quarters for the guest and his retinue." His eyes had already withdrawn, like the head of a Galapagos turtle into its enormous shell, and were remote, in contemplation of eternal verities piped up again.

"Ah, pardon me." The piercing stare of Ommodurad's eyes was on me again. "There was a friend of mine—swell guy, but impulsive. It seems he challenged the former Owner of Bar-Ponderone..."

Ommodurad did no more than twitch an eyebrow but suddenly the air was electric. His stare didn't waver by a millimeter but the lazy slouch of the six guards had altered to sprung steel. They hadn't moved but I felt them now all around me and not a foot away. I had a sinking feeling that I'd gone too far.

"—so I thought maybe I'd crave Your Excellency's help, if possible, to locate my pal," I finished weakly. For an interminable minute the Owner of Owners bored into me with his eyes. Then he raised a finger a quarter of an inch. The guards relaxed.

"Quarters for the guest and his retinue," repeated Ommodurad. He withdrew then...without moving. I was dismissed.

I went quietly, attended by my hulking escort.

I tried hard not to let my expression show any excitement, but I was feeling plenty.

Ommodurad was close mouthed for a reason. I was willing to bet that he had his memories of the Good Time intact.

Instead of the debased modern dialect that I'd heard; everywhere since my arrival, Ommodurad spoke flawless Old Vallonian.

IT was 27 o'clock and the Palace of Sapphires was silent. I was alone in the ornate bed chamber the Great Owner had assigned me. It was a nice room but I wouldn't learn anything staying in it. Nobody had said I was confined to quarters. I'd do a little scouting and see what I could pick up, if anything. I slung on the holster and .38 and slid out of the darkened chamber into the scarcely lighter corridor beyond. I saw a guard at the far end; he ignored me. I headed in the opposite direction.

None of the rooms were locked. There was no arsenal at the Palace and no archives that lesser folk than the Great Owner could use with profit. Everything was easy of access. I guessed that Ommadurad rightly counted on indifference to keep snoopers away. Here and there guards eyed me as I passed along but they said nothing.

I saw again by Cintelight the office where Ommadurad had received me and near it an ostentatious hall with black onyx floor and ceiling, gold hangings, and ceremonial ringboard. But the center of attraction was the familiar motif of the concentric circles of the Two Worlds, sketched in beaten gold across the broad wall of black marble behind the throne. Here the idea had been elaborated on. Outward from both the inner and outer circles flamed waving lines of sunburst, and at dead center a boss, like a sword hilt in form, chased in black and gold, erupted a foot from the wall. It was the first time I'd seen the symbol since I'd arrived on Vallon. I found it strangely exciting—like a footprint in the sand.

I went on, and came into a purple-vaulted hall where I saw a squad of guards, the same six who'd kept me such close company earlier in the day. They were drawn up at parade rest, three on each side of a massive ivory door. Somebody lived in safety and splendor on the other side.

Six sets of hard eyes turned my way. It was too late to duck back out of sight. I trotted up to the first of the row of guards. "Say, fella," I stage-whispered, "where's the ah—you know."

"Every bed chamber is equipped," he said gruffly, raising his sword and fingering its tip lovingly.

"Yeah? I never noticed." I moved off, looking chastened.

ON the ground floor I found Torbu and his cohort quartered in a barrack-room off the main entry hall. They had gotten hold of a few pipes of melon wine and were staging a small party with the help of several upstairs maids.

"We're still in enemy territory," I reminded Torbu. "I want every man ready. So save some of that booze for tomorrow."

"No fear, boss," said Torbu. "All my bullies got a eye on

the door and a hand on a knifehilt."

"Have you seen or heard anything useful?"

"Naw. These local dullards fall dumb at the first query."

"Keep your ears cocked. I want at least two men awake and on the alert all night."

"You bet, noble Drgon."

I judged distances carefully as I went back up the two flights to my own room. Inside I dropped into a brocaded easy chair and tried to add up what I'd seen.

First: Ommodurad's apartment, as nearly as I could judge, was directly over my own, two floors up. That was a break— or maybe I was where I was for easier surveillance. I'd skip that angle, I decided. It tended to discourage me and I needed all the enthusiasm I could generate.

Second: I wasn't going to learn anything useful trotting around corridors. Ommodurad wasn't the kind to leave traces of skullduggery lying around where the guests would see them.

And third: I should have known better than to hit this fortress with two squads and a .38 in the first place. Foster was here; Qohey had said so and the Great Owner's reaction to my mention of him confirmed it. What was it about Foster, anyway, that made him so interesting to these Top People? I'd have to ask him that when I found him. But to do that I'd have to leave the beaten track.

I went to the wide double window and looked up. A cloud swept from the great three-quarters face of Cinte, blue in the southern sky, and I could see an elaborately carved facade ranging up past a row of windows above my own to a railed balcony bathed in a pale light from the apartment within. If my calculations were correct that would be Ommodurad's digs. The front door was guarded like an octogenarian's harem but the back way looked like a breeze.

I pulled my head back in and thought about it. It was

risky...but it had that element of the unexpected that just might let me get away with it. Tomorrow the Owner of Owners' might have thought it through and switched me to another room...or to a cell in the basement. Then too, wall-scaling didn't occur to these Vallonians as readily as it did to a short-timer from Earth. They had too much to lose to risk it on a chancy climb.

Too much thinking is never a good idea when your pulse is telling you it's time for action. I rolled a heavy armoire fairly soundlessly over the deep-pile carpet and lodged it against the door. That might slow down a casual caller. I slipped the magazine out of the automatic, fitted nine greasy brass cartridges into it, slammed it home, dropped the pistol back in the holster. It had a comforting weight. I buttoned the strap over it and went back to the window.

THE clouds were back across Cinte's floodlight; that would help. I stepped out. The deep carving gave me easy handholds and I made it to the next windowsill without even working up a light sweat. Compared with my last climb, back in Lima, this was a cinch.

I rested a minute, then clambered around the dark window —just in case there was an insomniac on the other side of the glass—and went on up. I reached the balcony, had a hairy moment as I groped outward for a hold on the smooth floor-tiling above...and then I was pulling up and over the ornamental iron work.

The balcony was narrow, about twenty feet long, giving on half a dozen tall glass doors. Three showed light behind heavy drapes, three were dark. I moved close, tried to see something past the edge of the drapes. No go. I put an ear to the glass, thought maybe I heard a sound, like a distant volcano. That would be Ommodurad's brass rumble. The bear was in his cave.

I went along to the dark doors and on impulse tried a handle. It turned and the door swung in soundlessly. I felt my pulse pick up a double-time beat. I stood peering past the edge of the door into the ink-black interior. It didn't look inviting. In fact it looked as repellent as hell. Even a country boy like me could see that to step into the dragon's den without even a zippo to spot the footstools with would be the act of a nitwit.

I swallowed hard, got a firm grip on my pistol, and went in.

A soft fold of drapery brushed my face and I had the pistol out and my back to the wall with a speed that would have made Earp faint with envy. My adrenals gave a couple of wild jumps and my nervous system followed with a variety of sensations, none pleasant. I could hear Ommodurad's voice better now, muttering beyond the partition. If I could make out what he was saying...

I edged along the wall, found a heavy door, closed and locked. No help there. I felt my way further, found another door. Delicately I tried the handle.

A closet, half filled with racked garments. But I could hear more clearly now. Maybe it was a double closet with communicating doors to both the room I was in and the next one where the Great Owner was still rambling on. Apparently something had overcome his aversion to talking. There were pauses that must have been filled in by the replies of somebody else who didn't have the vocal timbre Ommodurad did.

I felt my way through the hanging clothing, felt over the closet walls. I was out of luck: there was no other door. I put an ear to the wall. I could catch an occasional word:

"...ring Okk-Hamiloth...vaults..."

IT sounded like something I'd like to hear more about.

How could I get closer? On impulse I reached up, touched a low ceiling...and felt a ridge like the trim around an access panel to a crawl space.

I crossed my fingers, stood on tiptoe to push at the panel. Nothing moved. I felt around in the dark, encountered a low shelf covered with shoes. I investigated; it was movable. I eased it aside a foot or two, piled the shoes on the floor, and stepped up.

The panel was two feet long on a side, with no discernible hinges or catch. I pushed some more, then gritted my teeth and heaved. There was a startlingly loud Crack! and the panel lifted. I blinked away the dust that settled in my eyes, reached to feel around within the opening, touched nothing but rough floor boards.

I cocked my head, listening. Ommodurad had stopped talking and another voice said something. Then there was a heavy thump, the clump of feet, and a metallic sound. After a moment the Great Owner's voice came again...and the other voice answered.

I stretched, grabbed the edge of the opening, and pulled myself up. I leaned forward, got a leg up, and rolled silently onto the rough floor. Feeling my way, I crawled, felt a wall rising, followed it, turned a corner... The voices were louder, quite suddenly. I saw why: there was a ventilating register ahead, gridded light gleaming through it. I crept along to the opening, lay flat, peered through it and saw three men.

Ommodurad was standing with his back to me, a giant figure swathed to the eyes in purple robes. Beside him a lean red-head with a leg that had been broken and badly stood round-shouldered, clutching a rod of office. The third man was Foster.

FOSTER stood, legs braced apart as though to withstand an earthquake, hands manacled before him. He looked steadily at the red-head, like a man marking a tree for cutting.

"I know nothing of these crimes," he said.

Ommodurad turned, swept out of sight. The red-head motioned. Foster turned away, moving stiffly, passed from my view. I heard a door open and close. I lay where I was and tried to sort out half a dozen conflicting impulses that clamored for attention. I finally decided it might do some good to gather more information. It had been bad luck that I had arrived at my peephole a few minutes too late to hear what the interview had been all about. But I might still make use of my strategic advantage.

I felt over the register, found fasteners at the corners. They lifted easily and the metal grating tilted back into my hands. I laid it aside, poked my head out. The room was empty, as far as I could see. It was time to take a few chances. I reversed my position, let my legs through the opening, and dropped softly to the floor. I reached back up and managed to prop the grating in position—just in case.

It was a fancy chamber, hung in purple and furnished for a king. I poked through the pigeon-holes of a secretary, opened a few cupboards, peered under the bed. It looked like I wasn't going to find any useful clues lying around loose.

I went to the glass doors to the balcony, unlocked one and left it ajar—in case I wanted to leave in a hurry. There was another door across the room. I went over and tried it; locked.

That gave me something definite to look for; a key. I rummaged some more in the secretary, then tried the drawer in a small table beside a broad couch and came up with a nice little steel key that looked like maybe...

I tried it. It was. Luck was still coming my way. I pushed open the door, saw a dark room beyond. I felt for a light switch, flicked it on, pushed the door shut behind me.

THE room looked like the popular idea of a necromancer's study. The windowless walls were lined with shelves packed close with books. The high black-draped ceiling hung like a hovering bat above the ramparted floor of bare, dark-polished wood. Narrow tables choked with books and instruments stood along a side of the chamber and at the far end I saw a deep-cushioned couch with a heavy dome-shaped apparatus like a beauty shop hair-dryer mounted at one end. I recognized it: it was a memory reinforcing machine, the first I had seen on Vallon.

I crossed the room and examined it. The last one I had seen—on the far-voyager in the room near the library—had been a stark utility model. This was a deluxe job, with soft upholstery and bright metal fittings and more dials and idiot lights than a late model Detroit status symbol. This solved one of the problems that had been hovering around the edge of my mind. I had fetched Foster's memory back to him but without a machine to use it in, it was just a tantalizing souvenir. Now all I had to do was sneak him away from Ommodurad, make it back here...

All of a sudden I felt tired, vulnerable, helpless and all alone. What was Ommodurad's interest in Foster? Why did he hide away here, keeping the rest of Vallon away with rumors of magic and spells? What connection did he have with the disaster that had befallen the Two Worlds—now reduced to One, and a poor one at that.

And why was I, a plain Joe named Legion, mixed up in it right to the eyebrows, when I could be sitting safe at home in a clean federal pen?

The answer to the last one wasn't too hard to recite; I had had a pal once, a smooth character named Foster, who had pulled me back from the ragged edge just when I was about to make a bigger mistake than usual. He had been a gentleman in the best sense of the word, and he had treated me like one. Together we had shared a strange adventure that had made me rich and had showed me that it was never too late to straighten your back and take on whatever the Fates handed out.

I had come running his way when trouble got too thick back home. And I'd found him in a worse spot than I was in. He had come back, after the most agonizing exile a man had ever suffered, to find his world fallen back into savagery, and his memory still eluding him. Now he was in chains, without friends and without hope...but still not broken, still standing on his own two feet...

But he was wrong on one point: he had one little hope. Not much: just a hard-luck guy with a penchant for bad decisions, but I was here and I was free. I had my pistol on my hip and a neat back way into the Owner's bedroom, and if I played it right and watched my timing and had maybe just a little luck, say about the amount it took to hit the Irish Sweepstakes, I might bring it off yet.

Right now it was time to return to my crawl-space. Ommodurad might come back and talk some more, tip me off to a vulnerable spot in the armor of his fortress. I went to the door, flicked off the light, turned the handle...and went rigid.


OMMODURAD was back. He pulled off the purple cloak, tossed it aside, strode to a wall bar. I clung to the crack of the door, not daring to move even to close it.

"But my lord," the voice of the red-head said, "I trow he remembers—"

"Not so," Ommodurad's voice rumbled. "On the morrow I strip his mind to the bare clean jelly..."

"Let me, dread lord. With my steel I'll have the truth o' him."

"Such a one as he your steel has never known!" the bass

voice snarled.

"Great Owner, I crave but one hour…tomorrow, in the Ceremonial Chamber. I shall environ him with the emblems of the past—"

"Enough!" Ommodurad's fist slammed against the bar, made glasses jump. "On such starveling lackwits as you a mighty empire hangs. It is a crime before the Gods and on his head I lay it." The Owner tossed off a glass. "I grant thy boon. Now begone, babbler of folly."

The red-head ducked, grinning, disappeared.

The big man threw off his clothes then. He clambered up on the wide couch, touched a switch somewhere, and the room was dark. Within five minutes I heard the heavy breathing of deep sleep.

I had found out one thing anyway: tomorrow was Foster's last day. One way or another Ommodurad and the red-head between them would destroy him. That didn't leave much time. But since the project was already hopeless it didn't make much difference.

I had a choice of moves now: I could tip-toe across to the register and try to wiggle through it without waking up the brontosaurus on the bed…or I could try for the balcony door a foot from where he slept…or I could stay put and wait him out. The last idea had the virtue of requiring no immediately daring adventures. I could just curl up on the floor, or, better still, on the padded couch…

A WEIRD idea was taking shape in my mind. I felt in my pocket, pulled out the two small cylinders that represented two men's memories of hundreds of years of living. One belonged to Foster, the one with the black and golden bands, but the other was the property of a stranger who had died three thousand years ago, out in space…

This cylinder, barely three inches long, held all the memories of a man who had been Foster's confidant when he was Qulqlan, a man who knew what had happened aboard the ship, what the purpose of the expedition had been, and what conditions they had left behind on Vallon.

I needed that knowledge. The cylinder could tell me plenty, including, possibly, the reason for Ommodurad's interest in Foster.

It was simple to use. I merely placed the cylinder in the receptacle in the side of the machine, took my place, lowered the helmet into position...and in an hour or so I would awaken with another man's memories stored in my brain, to use as I saw fit.

It would be a crime to waste the opportunity. The machine I had found here was probably the only one still in existence on Vallon. I had blundered my way into the one room in the palace that could help me in what I had to do; I had been lucky.

I went across to the soft cushioned chair. Looking it over carefully, I spotted the recess in its side, and thrust the plain cylinder into it.

I sat on the couch, lay back, reached up to pull the headpiece down into position, against my skull...

There was an instant of pain—like a prefrontal lobotomy performed without anesthetic.

Then blackness.

*I STOOD beside the royal couch where Qulqlan the Rthr lay and I saw that this was the hour for which I had waited long, for the Change was on him...*

*The time-scale stood at the third hour of the Death watch; all aboard slept save myself alone. I must move swiftly and at the Dawn watch show them the deed well done.*

*I shook the sleeping man, him who had once been the Rthr—king no more, by the law of the Change. He wakened slowly, looked about him, with the clear eyes of the newborn.*

*"Rise," I commanded: And the king obeyed.*

*"Follow me," I said. He made to question me, after the manner of those newly wakened from their Change. I bade him be silent. Like a lamb he came and I led him through shadowed ways to the cage of the Hunters. They rose, keen in their hunger, to my coming, as I had trained them.*

*I took the arm of Qulqlan and thrust it into the cage. The Hunters clustered, taking the mark of their prey. He watched, innocent eyes wide.*

*"That which you feel is pain, mindless one," I spoke. "It is a thing of which you will learn much in the time before you." Then they had done, and I set the time catch.*

*In my chambers I cloaked the innocent in a plain purple robe and afterward led him to the cradle where the lifeboat lay...*

*And by virtue of the curse of the Gods, which is upon me one was there before me. I waited not but moved as the haik strikes and took him fair in the back with my dagger. I dragged his body into hiding behind the flared foot of a column. But no sooner was he hidden well away than others came from the shadows, summoned by some device I know not of. They asked of the Rthr wherefore he walked by night, robed in the colors of Ammaerln of Bros-Ilyond. And I knew black despair that my grand design foundered thus in the shallows of their zeal.*

*Yet I spoke forth, with a great show of anger, that I, Ammaerln, vizier and companion to the Rthr, did but walk and speak in confidence with my liege lord.*

*But they persisted, Gholad foremost among them. And then one saw the hidden corse and in an instant they ringed me in.*

*THEN did I draw the long blade and hold it at the throat of Qulqlan. "Press me not, or your king will surely die," I said.*

*And they feared me and shrank back.*

*"Do you dream that I, Ammaerln, wisest of the wise, have come for*

*the love of far-voyaging?" I raged. "Long have I plotted against this hour; to lure the king a-voyaging in this his princely yacht, his faithful vizier at his side, that the Change might come on him far from his court. Then would the ancient wrong be redressed.*

*"There are those men born to rule as inevitably as the dream-tree seeks the sun—and such a one am I! Long has this one, now mindless, denied to me my destiny. But behold: I with a stroke shall set things aright.*

*"Below us lies a green world, peopled by savages. Not one am I to take blood vengeance on a man newborn from the Change. Instead I shall set him free to take up his life there below. May the Fates lead him again to royal state if that be their will—"*

*But there were naught but fools among them and they drew steel. I cried out to them that all, all should share!*

*But they heeded me not but rushed upon me. Then did I turn to Qulqlan and drive the long blade at his throat, but Gholad threw himself before him and fell, impaled in the throat. Then they pressed me and I did strike out against three who hemmed me close, and though they took many wounds they persisted in their madness, one leaping in to strike and another at my back, so that I whirled and slashed at shadows who danced away.*

*In the end I hunted them down in those corners whither they had dragged themselves and each did I put to the sword. And I turned at last to find the Rthr gone and some few with him, and madness took me that I had been gulled like a tinker by common men.*

*In the chamber of the memory couch would I find them. There they would seek to give back to the mindless one that memory of past glories which I had schemed so long to deny him. Almost I wept to see such cunning wasted. Terrible in my wrath I come upon them there. There were but two and, though they stood shoulder in the entry way, their poor dirks were no match for my long blade. I struck them dead and went to the couch, to lay my hand on the cylinder marked with the vile gold and black of Qulqlan, that I might destroy it and, with it, the Rthr, forever...*

*And I heard a sound and whirled about. A hideous figure staggered to me from the gloom and for an instant I saw the flash of steel in the bloody hand of the accursed Gholad whom I had left for dead. Then I knew cold agony between my ribs...*

GHOLAD *lay slumped against wall, his face greenish above the blood-soaked tunic. When he spoke air whistled through his slashed throat.*

*"Have done, traitor who once was honored of the king," he whispered. "Have you no pity for him who once ruled in justice and splendor at High Okk-Hamiloth?"*

*"Had you not robbed me of my destiny, murderous dog," I croaked, "that splendor would have been mine."*

*"You came upon him helpless," gasped Gholad. "Make some amends now for your shame. Let the Rthr have his mind, which is more precious than his life."*

*"I but rest to gather strength. Soon will I rise and turn him from the couch. Then will I die content."*

*"Once you were his friend," Gholad whispered. "By his side you fought, when both of you were young. Remember that...and have pity. To leave him here, in this ship of death, mindless and alone..."*

*"I have loosed the Hunters!" I shrieked in triumph. "With them will the Rthr share this tomb until the end of time!"*

*Then I searched within me and found a last terrible strength and I rose up...and even as my hand reached out to pluck away the mind trace of the king I felt the bloody fingers of Gholad on my ankle, and then my strength was gone. And I was falling headlong into that dark well of death from, which there is no returning...*

\* \* \*

I woke up and lay for a long time in the dark without moving, trying to remember the fragments of a strange dream of violence and death. I could still taste the lingering dregs of some bitter emotion. For a moment I couldn't remember what it was I had to do; then with a start I recalled where I was. I had lain down on the couch and pulled the headpiece into place—

It hadn't worked.

I thought hard, tried to tap a new reservoir of memories, drew a blank. Maybe my Earth-mind was too alien for the Vallonian memory trace to affect. It was another good idea that hadn't worked out. But at least I had had a good rest. Now it was time to get moving. First: to see if Ommodurad was still asleep. I started to sit up—

Nothing happened.

I had a moment of vertigo, as my inner ear tried to accommodate to having stayed in the same place after automatically adjusting to my intention of rising. I lay perfectly still and tried to think it through.

I had tried to move...and hadn't so much as twitched a muscle, I was paralyzed...or tied up...or maybe, if I was lucky, imagining things. I could try it again and next time—

I was afraid to try. Suppose I tried and nothing happened —again? This was ridiculous. All I had to do was sit up. I—

Nothing, I lay in the dark and tried to will an arm to move, my head to turn. It was as though I had no arm, no head— just a mind, alone in the dark. I strained to sense the ropes that held me down; still nothing. No ropes, no arms, no body. There was no pressure against me from the couch, no vagrant itch or cramp, no physical sensation. I was a disembodied brain, lying nestled in a great bed of pitch-black cotton wool.

Then, abruptly, I was aware of myself—not the gross mechanism of clumsy bone and muscle, but the neuro-electric field generated within the massive structure of a brain alive with flashing currents and a lightning interplay of molecular forces. A sense of orientation grew. I occupied a block of cells...here in the left hemisphere. The mass of neural tissue loomed over me, gigantic. And "I"..."I" was reduced to the elemental ego, who possessed as a material appurtenance 'my' arms and legs, 'my' body, 'my' brain... Relieved of outside stimuli I was able now to conceptualize myself as I actually was: an insubstantial state existing in an immaterial continuum, created by the action of neural currents within the cerebrum, as a magnetic field is created in space by the flow of electricity.

And I knew what had happened, I had opened my mind to invasion by alien memories. The other mind had seized upon the sensory centers, driven me to this dark corner. I was a fugitive within my own skull.

For a timeless time I lay stunned, immured now as the massive stones of Bar-Ponderone had never confined me. My basic self-awareness still survived, but was shunted aside, cut off from any contact with the body itself.

With shadowy fingers of imagination I clawed at the walls surrounding me, fought for a glimpse of light, for a way out.

And found none.

Then, at last, I began again to think.

I must analyze my awareness of my surroundings, seek out channels through which impulses from sensory nerves flowed, and tap them.

I tried cautiously; an extension of my self-concept reached out with ultimate delicacy. There were the ranked infinities of cells, there the rushing torrents of gross fluid, there the taut cables of the interconnecting web, and there—

Barrier! Blank and impregnable the wall reared up. My questing tendril of self-stuff raced over the surface like an ant over a melon, and found no tiniest fissure.

I withdrew. To dissipate my forces was senseless. I must

select a point of attack, hurl against it all the power of my surviving identity.

The last of the phantom emotions that had clung—for how long? —to the incorporeal mind field had faded now, leaving me with no more than an intellectual determination to reassert myself. Dimly I recognized this sign of my waning sense of identity but there was no surge of instinctive fear. Instead I coolly assessed my resources—and almost at once stumbled into an unused channel, here within my own self-field. For a moment I recoiled from the outer configuration of the stored patterns...and then I remembered.

I had been in the water, struggling, while the Red soldier waited, rifle aimed. And then: a flood of data, flowing with cold, impersonal precision. And I had deftly marshaled the forces of my body to survive.

And once more: as I hung by numbed fingers under the cornice of the Yordano Tower, the cold voice had spoken.

And I had forgotten. The miracle had been pushed back, rejected by the conscious mind. But now I knew: this was the knowledge that I had received from the background briefing device that I had used in my island strong-room before I fled. This was the survival data known to all Old Vallonians of the days of the Two Worlds. It had lain here, unused; the secrets of superhuman strength and endurance... buried by the imbecile censor-self's aversion to the alien.

But it was the ego alone that remained now, stripped of the burden of neurosis, freed from any and all subconscious pressures. The levels of the mind were laid completely bare, and I saw close at hand the regions where dreams were born, the barren sources of instinctive fear-patterns, the linkages to the blinding emotions; and all lay now under my overt control.

Without further hesitation I tapped the stored Vallonian

knowledge, encompassed it, made it mine. There again I approached the barrier, spread out across it, probed in vain—

"*...vile primitive...*"

The thought thundered out with crushing force. I recoiled, then renewed my attack, alert now, I knew what to do.

I sought and found a line of synaptic weakness, burrowed at it—

"*...intolerable...vestigial...erasure...*"

I struck instantly, slipped past the impervious shield, laid firm hold on the optic receptor bank. The alien mind threw itself against me, but too late. I held secure and the assault faded, withdrew. Cautiously I extended my interpretive receptivity. There was a pattern of pulses, oscillations in the lambda/mu range. I tuned, focussed—

Abruptly I was seeing. For a moment my fragile equilibrium tottered, as I strove to integrate the flow of external stimuli into my bodiless self-concept. Then a balance was struck: I held my ground and stared through the one eye I had recaptured from the usurper.

And I reeled again!

Bright daylight blazed in the chamber of Ommodurad. The scene shifted as the body moved about, crossing the room, turning...I had assumed that the body still lay in the dark but instead, it walked, without my knowledge, propelled by a stranger.

The field of vision flashed across the couch, Ommodurad was gone.

I sensed that the entire left lobe, disoriented by the loss of the eye, had slipped now to secondary awareness, its defenses weakened. I retreated momentarily from my optic outpost, laid a temporary traumatic block across the access nerves to keep the intruder from reasserting possession, and concentrated my force in an attack on the auricular channels.

It was an easy rout.   I seized on the nerve trunk, then instantly reoccupied the eye, coordinated its impressions with those coming in along the aural nerves...and heard my voice mouth a curse.

The body was standing beside a bare wall with a hand laid upon it.  In the wall a recess partly obscured by a sliding panel stood empty.

The body turned, strode to a doorway, emerged into a gloomy violet-shadowed corridor.  The glance flicked from the face of one guard to another.  They stared in open-mouthed surprise, brought weapons up.

"You dare to bar the path to the Lord Ammaerln?" My voice slashed at the men.  "Stand aside, as you value your lives."

And the body pushed past them, strode off along the corridor.  It passed through a great archway, descended a flight of marble stairs, came along a hall I had seen on my tour of the Palace of Sapphires and into the Onyx Chamber with the great golden sunburst that covered the high black wall.

In the Great Owner's chair at the ringboard Ommodurad sat scowling at the lame courtier whose red hair was hidden now under a black cowl.  Between them Foster stood, the heavy manacles dragging at his wrists.

Ommodurad turned; his face paled, then flush dark rose, teeth bared.

The gaze of my eye fixed on Foster.  Foster stared back, a look of incredulity growing on his face.

"My Lord Rthr," my voice said.  The eye swept down and fixed on the manacles.  The body drew back a step, as if in horror.

"You overreach yourself, Ommodurad!" my voice cried harshly.

Ommodurad stepped toward me, his immense arm raised.

"Lay not a hand on me, dog of a usurper!" my voice roared out. "By the Gods, would you take me for common clay!"

And, unbelievably, Ommodurad paused, stared in my face.

"I know you as the upstart Drgon, petty Owner," he rumbled. "But I trow I see another there behind your pale eyes."

"Foul was the crime that brought me to this pass," my voice said. "But...know that your master, Ammaerln, stands before you, in the body of a primitive!"

"Ammaerln...!" Ommodurad jerked as though he had been struck.

My body turned, dismissing him. The eye rested on Foster.

"My liege," my voice said unctuously. "I swear the dog dies for this treason—"

"It is a mindless one, intruder," Ommodurad broke in. "Seek no favor with the Rthr, for he that was Rthr is no more. You deal with me now."

My body whirled on Ommodurad. "Give a thought to your tone, lest your ambitions prove your death!"

Ommodurad put a hand to his dagger. "Ammaerln of Bros-Ilyond you may be, or a changeling from dark regions I know not of. But know that this day I hold all power in Vallon."

"And what of this one who was once Qulqlan? What consort do you hold with him you say is mindless?" I saw my hand sweep out in a contemptuous gesture at Foster.

"An end to patience!" the Great Owner roared. He started toward my body.

"Does the fool, Ommodurad, forget the power of the great Ammaerln?" my voice said softly and the towering figure hesitated once more, searching my face. "The Rthr's hour is past...and so is yours, bungler and fool. Your self-delusion is ended." My voice rose in a bellow: "Know that I...Ammaerln, the great...have returned to rule at High Okk-Hamiloth...

He threw back his head, and laughed a choked throaty laugh that was half sob.

"Know, demon, or madman, or ancient prince of evil: for thirty centuries have I brooded alone, sealed from an empire by a single key!"

I felt the shock rack through and through the invader mind. This was the opportunity I had hoped for. Quick as thought I moved, slashed at the wavering shield, and was past it—

Upon the mind-picture of Foster's face was now superimposed another: that of Qulqlan, Rthr of all Vallon, ruler of the Two Worlds!

And other pictures, snatched from the intruder mind, were present now in the Earth-consciousness of me, Legion:

the vaults, deep in the rock under the fabled city of Okk-Hamiloth, where the mind-trace of every citizen was stored, sealed by the Rthr and keyed to his mind alone;

Ammaerln, urging the king to embark on a far-voyage, stressing the burden of government, tempting him to bring with him the royal mind-trace;

Qulqlan's acquiescence and Ammaerln's secret joy at the advancement of his scheme;

the coming of the Change for the Rthr, aboard ship, far out in space and the vizier's bold stroke;

and then the fools who found him at the lifeboat...and the loss of all, all...

There my own lived memories took up the tale: the awakening of Foster, unsuspecting, and his recording of the mind of the dying Ammaerln; the flight from the Hunters;

the memory trace of the king, that lay for three millennia among neolithic bones until I, a mere primitive, plucked it from its place; and the pocket of a coarse fibre garment where the cylinder lay now, on a hip of the body I inhabited and as inaccessible to me as if it had been a million miles away.

But there was a second memory trace—Ammaerln. I had crossed a galaxy to come to Foster, and with me, locked in an unmarked pewter cylinder, I had brought Foster's ancient nemesis.

I had given it life, and a body.

Foster, once Rthr, had survived against all logic and had come back from the dead: the last hope of a golden age...

To meet his fate at my hands.

"Three thousand years," I heard my voice saying, "Three thousand years have the men of Vallon lived mindless, with the power that was Vallon locked away in a vault without a key. And now, you think to force this mind—that is no mind —to unseal the vault?"

"I know it for a hopeless task," Ommodurad said. "At first I thought—since he speaks the tongue of old Vallon— that he dissembled. But he knows nothing. This is but the dry husk of the Rthr...and I sicken of the sight. I would fain kill him now and let the long farce end."

"Not so!" my voice cut in. "Once I decreed exile to the mindless one. So be it!"

The face of Ommodurad twisted in its rage. "Your witless chatterings! I tire of them."

"Wait!" my voice snarled. "Would you put aside the key?"

There was a silence as Ommodurad stared at my face. I saw my hand rise into view. Gripped in it was Foster's memory trace.

"The Two Worlds lie in my hand," my voice spoke.

"Observe well the black and golden bands of the royal memory trace. Who holds this key is all-powerful. As for the mindless body yonder, let it be destroyed."

Ommodurad locked eyes with mine. Then, "Let the deed be done," he said.

The red-head drew a long stiletto from under his cloak, smiling, I could wait no longer...

Along the link I had kept through the intruder's barrier I poured the last of the stored energy of my mind. I felt the enemy recoil, then strike back with crushing force. But I was past the shield.

As the invader reached out to encircle me I shattered my unified forward impulse into myriad nervous streamlets that flowed on, under, over, and around the opposing force; I spread myself through and through the inner mass, drawing new power from the trunk sources.

Now! I struck for the right optic center, clamped down with a death grip.

The enemy mind went mad as the darkness closed in. I heard my voice scream and I saw in vivid pantomime the vision that threatened the invader: the redhead darting, the stiletto flashing—

And then the invading mind broke, swirled into chaos, and was gone...

I reeled, shocked and alone inside my skull. The brain loomed, dark and untenanted now. I began to move, crept along the major nerve paths, reoccupied the cortex—

Agony! I twisted, felt again with a massive return of sensation my arms, my legs, opened both eyes to see blurred figures moving. And in my chest a hideous pain...

I was sprawled on the floor, I lay gasping. Sudden understanding came: the red-head had struck...and the other mind, in full rapport with the pain centers, had broken under the shock, left the stricken brain to me alone.

As through a red veil I saw the giant figure of Ommodurad loom, stoop over me, rise with the royal cylinder in his hand. And beyond, Foster strained backward, the chain between his wrists garroting the red-head. Ommodurad turned, took a step, flicked the man from Foster's grasp and hurled him aside. He drew his dagger. Quick as a hunting cat Foster leaped, struck with the manacles...and the knife clattered across the floor. Ommodurad backed away with a curse, while the red-head seized the stiletto he had let fall and moved in. Foster turned to meet him, staggering, and raised heavy arms.

I fought to move, got my hand as far as my side, fumbled with the leather strap. The alien mind had stolen from my brain the knowledge of the cylinder but I had kept from it the fact of the pistol. I had my hand on its butt now. Painfully I drew it, dragged my arm up, struggled to raise the weapon, centered it on the back of the mop of red hair, free now of the cowl...and fired.

Ommodurad had found his dagger. He turned back from the corner where Foster had sent it spinning. Foster retreated until his back was at the wall. My vision grew dimmer. The great gold circles of the Two Worlds seemed to revolve, while waves of darkness rolled over me.

But there was a thought: something I had found among the patterns in the intruder's mind. At the center of the sunburst rose a boss, in black and gold, erupting a foot from the wall, like a sword-hilt...

The thought came from far away. The sword of the Rthr, used once, in the dawn of a world, by a warrior king but laid away now, locked in its sheath of stone, keyed to the mind-pattern of the Rthr, that none other might ever draw it to some ignoble end.

A sword, keyed to the basic mind-pattern of the king...

I drew one last breath and blinked back the darkness. Ommodurad stepped past me, knife in hand, toward the unarmed man.

"Foster," I croaked. "The sword..."

Foster's head came up. I had spoken in English; the syllables rang strangely in that outworld setting, Ommodurad ignored the unknown words.

"Draw...the sword...from the stone! ...You're... Qulqlan...Rthr...of Vallon."

I saw him reach out, grasp the ornate hilt, Ommodurad, with a cry, leaped toward him—

The sword slid out smoothly, four feet of glittering steel. Ommodurad stopped, stared at the manacled hands gripping the hilt of the fabled blade. Slowly he sank to his knees, bent his neck.

"I yield, Qulqlan," he said. "I crave the mercy of the Rthr."

Behind me I heard thundering feet. Dimly I was aware of Torbu raising my head, of Foster leaning over me. They were saying something but I couldn't hear. My feet were cold, and the coldness crept higher. The winds that swept through eternity blew away the last shred of ego and I was one with darkness...

# EPILOGUE

I awoke to a light like that of a morning when the world was young. Gossamer curtains fluttered at tall windows, through which I saw a squadron of trim white clouds riding in a high blue sky.

I turned my head, and Foster stood beside me, dressed in a short white tunic.

"That's a crazy set of threads, Foster," I said, "but on your build it looks good. But you've aged; you look twenty-five if you look a day."

Foster smiled. "Welcome to Vallon, my friend," he said in English.

"Vallon," I said. "Then it wasn't all a dream?"

"Regard it as a dream, Legion. Your life begins today," Someone came forward from behind Foster.

"Gope," I said. Then I hesitated. "You are Gope, aren't you?" I said in Vallonian.

He laughed.

"I was known by that name once," he said, "but my true name is Gwanne."

My eyes fell on my legs. I saw that I was wearing a tunic like Foster's except that mine was different. It was a pale blue.

"Who put the dress on me?" I asked. "And where's my

pants?"

"This garment suits you better," said Gope. "Come. Look in the glass."

I got to my feet, stepped to a long mirror, glanced at the reflection. "It's not the real me, boys," I started. Then I stared, open-mouthed. A Hercules, black-haired and clean-limbed, stared back. I shut my mouth...and his mouth shut. I moved an arm and he did likewise. I whirled around to Foster.

"What...how...who...?"

"The mortal body that was Legion died of its wounds," he said, "but the mind that was within the man was recorded. We have waited many, many years to give that mind life again."

I turned back to the mirror, gaped. The young giant gaped back. "I remember," I said, "I remember...a knife...a knife in my guts...and a red-headed man...and the Great Owner, and..."

"For his crimes," told Gope, "he went to a place of exile until the Change should come on him. Long have we waited."

I looked again and now I saw two faces in the mirror and both of them were young. One was low down, just above my ankles, and it belonged to a cat I had known as Itzenca. The other, higher up, was that of a man I had known as Ommodurad. But this was a clear-eyed Ommodurad, just under twenty-one.

"Onto the blank slate we traced your mind," said Gope.

"He owed you a life, Legion," Foster said. "His own was forfeit."

"I guess I ought to kick and scream and demand my original ugly puss back," I said slowly, studying my reflection for a few moments, "but the fact is, I like looking like Mr.

Universe."

"Your earthly body was infected with the germs of old age," said Foster. "Now you can look forward to a great span of life."

"But come," said Gope. "All Vallon waits to honor you." He led the way to the tall window.

"Your place is by my side at the great ringboard," said Foster. "And afterwards: all of the Two Worlds lie before you."

I looked past the open window and saw a carpet of velvet green that curved over foothills to the rim of a forest. Down the long sward I saw a procession of bright knights and ladies come riding on animals, some black, some golden palamino, that looked for all the world like unicorns.

My eyes traveled upward to where the light of a great white sun flashed on blue towers. And somewhere in the distance trumpets sounded.

"It looks like a pretty fair offer," I said.

## THE END

*If you've enjoyed this book, you will not want to miss these terrific titles...*

## ARMCHAIR SCI-FI, FANTASY, & HORROR DOUBLE NOVELS, $12.95 each

**D-1**    **THE GALAXY RAIDERS** by William P. McGivern
       **SPACE STATION #1** by Frank Belknap Long

**D-2**    **THE PROGRAMMED PEOPLE** by Jack Sharkey
       **SLAVES OF THE CRYSTAL BRAIN** by William Carter Sawtelle

**D-3**    **YOU'RE ALL ALONE** by Fritz Leiber
       **THE LIQUID MAN** by Bernard C. Gilford

**D-4**    **CITADEL OF THE STAR LORDS** by Edmund Hamilton
       **VOYAGE TO ETERNITY** by Milton Lesser

**D-5**    **IRON MEN OF VENUS** by Don Wilcox
       **THE MAN WITH ABSOLUTE MOTION** by Noel Loomis

**D-6**    **WHO SOWS THE WIND...** by Rog Phillips
       **THE PUZZLE PLANET** by Robert A. W. Lowndes

**D-7**    **PLANET OF DREAD** by Murray Leinster
       **TWICE UPON A TIME** by Charles L. Fontenay

**D-8**    **THE TERROR OUT OF SPACE** by Dwight V. Swain
       **QUEST OF THE GOLDEN APE** by Ivar Jorgensen and Adam Chase

**D-9**    **SECRET OF MARRACOTT DEEP** by Henry Slesar
       **PAWN OF THE BLACK FLEET** by Mark Clifton.

**D-10**    **BEYOND THE RINGS OF SATURN** by Robert Moore Williams
       **A MAN OBSESSED** by Alan E. Nourse

## ARMCHAIR SCIENCE FICTION CLASSICS, $12.95 each

**C-1**    **THE GREEN MAN**
       by Harold M. Sherman

**C-2**    **A TRACE OF MEMORY**
       By Keith Laumer

## ARMCHAIR MASTERS OF SCIENCE FICTION SERIES, $16.95 each

**M-1**    **MASTERS OF SCIENCE FICTION, Vol. One**
       Bryce Walton—"Dark of the Moon" and other tales

**M-2**    **MASTERS OF SCIENCE FICTION, Vol. Two**
       Jerome Bixby: "One Way Street" and other tales